NAILED!!!

Shirley Lerch Crum

PublishAmerica
Baltimore

First printing

At the specific preference of the author, PublishAmerica allowed this work to remain exactly as the author intended, verbatim, without editorial input.

ISBN: 1-4241-2399-2
PUBLISHED BY PUBLISHAMERICA, LLLP
www.publishamerica.com
Baltimore

Printed in the United States of America

Dedication

To Mom on her 90th year,

To the Angels in Heaven—
    especially Dad, whose smile could light up my heart,
    and Katy, who will forever more be seven years old,

And to those other Angels who wait patiently for me—
    my dog Sarah, the most faithful companion a woman could ever
    have,
    and Little Bit, my "Doc."

Acknowledgments

Thanks to my husband Michael for his hours of editing, and to Boombalatti's Homemade Ice Cream and Tavernay's Jewelers for allowing me to use their names for a touch of realism.

Thanks also to Colette Teachey, Kirsten Holmstedt, and Linda Douglas for helping me spread the word of hope.

Finally, for their continued support, my thanks go to the readers at the Holly Tree Retirement Community and to Reverend Linda Taylor and the members of Oleander United Methodist Church.

Prologue

Java Joe's
The Third Week in November
Saturday Morning

Carl Austin, Cutthroat Carl to those who had the dubious pleasure of dealing with him, sat slouched in a black wrought-iron chair, in the shade of a green and white umbrella perched above an outside table at Java Joe's. His wide-brimmed Panama hat and white suit seemed out of place in the bright but brisk autumn day. He sipped a double mocha latte and watched the traffic on Military Cutoff Road come to a standstill as the light changed from yellow to red. Suddenly the cell phone on the table in front of him began to crow like a rooster and vibrate, causing it to bounce around the table. Flipping the phone open, he scanned the surroundings for anyone who could possibly listen in. Assured of privacy, he answered simply, "Yes."

"Our friend has come to the unfortunate attention of others."

Carl uncrossed his legs, sat up, and scowled, shifting the phone to his other ear. "Why? His cover has worked so perfectly up to now. What happened?"

"Our friend is a fool. He has gotten himself mixed up with a woman who just happens to work part-time for the FBI."

The scowl deepened. "Is she on to him? Has our mission been compromised?"

"We don't think so, although you'll have to be sure." The voice on the other end laughed a joyless laugh. "No, ironically, it's the man she dated before him that has caused the problem. It seems he is still interested in her and has been nosing around."

Carl took another sip of his latte. "Maybe we should eliminate him."

The disembodied voice growled ominously. "No way! The man is regular FBI. We touch him and the whole operation could unravel. Better to just arrange an accident for our friend. Then there will be no link to us. Besides, the good professor has finished what we needed him to do. He has outlived his usefulness to us. But remember, it must look like an accident."

"What about the woman?"

The voice hesitated. "Use your own judgment."

Silence followed. Finally, a satisfied smile spread across Carl's face. "Don't worry. I think I have a plan that will alleviate all our problems."

Chapter One

Reva's-on-the-River
Downtown Wilmington, NC
The Third Week in November
Sunday Afternoon

"I can't believe your wedding is only one month away," gushed Cathy as she squeezed Linda's hand. They were seated at a front window table inside Reva's-on-the-River Restaurant, located in the heart of downtown Wilmington. From their vantage point the two could see the USS North Carolina floating majestically on the Cape Fear River. Today, neither of them paid any attention to it. Linda Tate, a computer analyst for an international company when not needed by the FBI, had come into town from Raleigh for the weekend to have a fitting for her bridal gown and to see to more wedding details.

The bride's bright green eyes sparkled as she grinned at Cathy Cleveland, her best friend since college. This would be Linda's first trip down the aisle. Her one and only other love had died tragically in an unfortunate accident years before. "Well C.C., if you would have told me last June that, within a month, I would meet a distinguished airline captain named David Sokol, fall in love, get engaged, almost lose my life to a bunch of diamond smugglers, move to Raleigh from Chicago, and go to work undercover for the FBI, I would have called you crazy."

"I've got to agree with you. Never in my wildest imagination did I dream that our lives would take such a dramatic turn. And to think that it's just been since that fateful Disney World trip in July." Cathy's brown eyes twinkled in return. "All I can say is thank goodness you have such a thing for scarves. If Peter hadn't spotted yours in the car that awful day, who knows what would have happened to us. Incidentally, I love the scarf you have on today. It matches your outfit perfectly."

Linda touched the lavender silk scarf that encircled her throat. "Thanks," then shifting in her chair, she continued, "Getting back to July, I don't even like to think about where we'd be right now if Peter hadn't shown up when he did." Momentarily lost in thought, Linda broke the suddenly somber mood with laughter. "I really didn't think you or I would survive the FBI training at Quantico."

"Hey, for a couple of ladies in our mid-forties, I think we did just fine," Cathy shot back in mock indignation. Thinking back over the events of the last few months, the woman's eyes again sobered. She stared at her glass and swirled the straw around in the unsweetened iced tea. Unconsciously touching the front of her shirt with slightly trembling fingers and catching her lower lip between slightly uneven teeth, the college instructor abruptly changed the subject: "I'm sorry that my matron-of-honor gown had to be redesigned because of my chest, or should I say lack of. It's just that I haven't worn any prostheses since Disney World, and I just wouldn't be comfortable in them now."

Now it was Linda's turn to squeeze Cathy's hand. "Don't worry about it, C.C. I admire you for not giving in to society's pressure to have reconstructive surgery after your mastectomies or, for that matter, to wear prostheses."

Cathy glanced at her friend and shrugged. "Once I stopped wearing the breast prostheses, the only person who blatantly stared at my chest was the division chair for the sciences, Dr. Moran. At the opening faculty meeting in August, his eyes never left the front of my blouse. I was tempted to rip the thing off and say, 'Here, take a picture why don't you!'"

The computer analyst shook her head and grimaced. They sat in companionable silence for a few more minutes before Linda shifted the conversation to what she assumed was a happier subject: "I'm sorry I didn't get to see Peter this weekend. How are you and he doing?" Hoping to elicit a grin from her matron of honor, the bride-to-be giggled, "I thought there for awhile that you and I might have a double wedding ceremony." Peter was Peter Channing of the FBI, whom Cathy had met when he, his late wife, and Cathy had attended the same cancer support group years before in Chicago. They renewed their friendship when Cathy asked for his help in Florida.

Instead of providing the hoped-for grin, Cathy gazed at her friend and hesitated a moment before quietly answering, "Disney World is such a magical place that we kind of got carried away last summer. When reality returned, I realized that things were happening a little too fast for me. We decided to slow it down."

A delicately arched left eyebrow shot up a fraction of an inch. "By we, do you mean you and Peter, or did you decide to slow it down all by yourself?" When Cathy didn't immediately answer but instead shifted her attention out the window, Linda's left eyebrow rose even higher. "I know Peter is crazy about you, and I thought you felt the same about him. Why am I suddenly sensing reluctance on your part? What's changed?" There was still no answer. Linda's voice raised a notch with a tone of total exasperation. "Don't tell me it's once again because of your ex. Look, he was a jerk. As far as I am concerned, any middle-aged man who leaves his wife for his twenty-something-year-old secretary should be forced to sit in a vat of ice-cold water for a month."

Cathy grinned in spite of herself, then quickly sobered and vehemently shook her head. "With the way I treated him after the first mastectomy, I told you he had every right to leave. But that is not the point." She leaned far forward. "The point is that my ex has nothing to do with what is going on now."

The computer analyst tilted her head to one side, leaned back, and folded her arms across her chest. "Then I repeat my question: What's changed?"

C.C. rubbed her chin with her right hand as she looked into the eyes of her best friend. "The truth?"

Linda leaned far forward. "Of course!"

With face slightly flushed, eyes cast downward, and drawing imaginary designs on her plate with a dinner knife, slowly, almost reluctantly, Cathy answered, "There is a visiting physics professor by the name of John Marley who lectured at the college a few weeks ago. The professor has written several books and is really quite amazing." With growing enthusiasm, she warmed to her subject. Once again meeting the eyes of her friend and appearing almost giddy, C.C.'s speech became more rapid. "The man travels to colleges and universities throughout the country and gives guest lectures. The students just love him. Right in front of them, John does crazy things like walking on hot coals. He even lies between beds of nails and has a student pile on concrete blocks and hit them with a sledgehammer. He demonstrates dozens of other principles of physics as well. This guy makes science come alive for the students. Believe me, he's incredible." Using his first name quite freely now, Cathy continued, "John's been in the eastern Carolinas for about a month, traveling between the various colleges along the coast."

Linda stabbed her grilled king mackerel steak with her fork, almost afraid of where this conversation was heading. "And?"

Her friend sighed and slowed down. "And, to make a long story short, we've been seeing quite a lot of each other since he came to town. While lecturing throughout this area, he's made Wilmington his home base. John is charming, witty, and smart. We have a great time together."

Linda sat, open-mouthed, now slouched far back in her chair as if pinned there by the words just heard. "Why didn't you say anything before this?" When Cathy wasn't quick to answer, she straightened up, trying to read her friend's eyes. "Don't tell me that you are in love with him?"

Cathy lowered her eyes and shook her head unconvincingly. "No. Besides, he's leaving next week." Again meeting her best friend's gaze, C.C.'s tone became earnestly intense: "But don't you see?

That's not the point. The point is that if I truly loved Peter, I don't think I'd want to spend so much time with John, now would I? And I didn't say anything sooner because I know how much both you and David like Peter." With that, she sat back and folded her arms defiantly.

Dumbfounded and staring at her friend, both of the computer analyst's eyebrows rose. "I honestly don't know what to say. Does Peter know how you feel?"

Cathy sighed and rolled her eyes. "Oh, yes. Remember, I teach communication. I know how important it is to talk honestly, so I've been completely up front about all this with him." Her tone softened a little. "Don't get me wrong—I still care a great deal about Peter. We still go out occasionally, just not every weekend."

"Peter Channing is a wonderful man whose FBI training saved both our lives. I know he loves you and is the one man who, after losing his own wife to that horrible disease, truly understands what you went through and, for that matter, are still going through because of the breast cancer. Not to mention the fact that, at almost six feet tall, with his closely-cropped salt-and-pepper beard and moustache and incredibly piercing blue eyes, that agent happens to be extremely handsome." Quickly raising her hand as if to stop any protest from Cathy, she continued, "The bald spot on the top of his head only goes to make him even more dashing. What more could you want?" When Cathy refused to answer, Linda paused and searched the eyes of the woman seated across the table. "Think long and hard before you do something you might regret for the rest of your life."

The cloud that covered Cathy's face lifted, replaced by an impish half grin. Crossing her heart with the finger of her right hand, she teasingly replied, "I promise." Sensing that her best friend was still upset, she tried again to lighten the mood. "Gee, with the way you describe Peter, are you sure you are not in love with him instead of your airline pilot? After all, Captain David Sokol is quite a hunk himself, with his eyes the color of a storm-tossed sea, hair that makes me think of a gray fox, and that five-foot ten-inch solidly built frame.

Come to think of it, if you don't want him, I'll take him." The tension finally snapped as both women laughed merrily.

"Not a chance. I know what I got and I intend to keep him! Thank you very much." Captain Sokol's future bride stretched. "This weekend has been a lot of fun."

Cathy glanced down at her watch. "We better get a move on if you're going to get back to Raleigh by dinner."

They walked arm-in-arm out to Linda's car. Linda opened the door, then turned and hugged her friend. From her petite five feet two inches, she looked up at Cathy towering above her at almost five feet eight. "Be careful, C.C., that's all I'm saying."

"I will. I promise. Give that man of yours a hug for me. And tell him I'll expect both of you down here next weekend for Thanksgiving."

As Cathy turned to leave, a dark sedan careened around the corner and barreled toward them. Linda grabbed her friend's arm and pulled backward, spilling both women into the driver's seat of the sea-foam green VW bug.

By the time the women untangled themselves from the front seat of the bug, the dark sedan was long gone. "Are you all right?" Linda asked Cathy anxiously.

"Just a little shaken. What about you?"

"About the same," the analyst answered, smoothing out her now disheveled clothes. "Boy, you sure have some idiot drivers in this town."

"Don't I know it. The very first month I moved down here I was rear-ended by a young woman talking on a cell phone while taking notes on a laptop, all the while driving a pick-up truck." Cathy stared in the direction of the now vanished car. "Still, if I didn't know better, I'd swear that car purposely swerved to hit us."

"Why, on earth, would anyone want to do that?"

"I haven't a clue."

Linda cocked her head at her friend, "Don't tell anybody, but I think you're being a little paranoid!"

"You're probably right." Focusing again on the petite woman in front of her, Cathy asked skeptically, "Are you going to be okay driving back to Raleigh after that?"

"Sure. I'm fine. Remember, as a computer analyst I'm extremely left-brained. That means I'm more logical and far less emotional than you are, Ms. Right Brain. As far as I'm concerned, that incident is already over and done."

Cathy watched Linda drive away and took a deep, ragged breath. She really was a lot more emotional than Linda, and it seemed doubly true since the cancer. Ordering herself to focus on something else, she checked her watch again. John would be meeting her in an hour in the physics lab at Ekim College, a small private school also located in the heart of downtown Wilmington. The visiting professor was scheduled to finish up a guest lecture series there, then head to California the day after Thanksgiving. Cathy didn't want to think about his leaving now. Tonight they were to attend a play at Thalian Hall, the beautiful historic theater located at the heart of downtown Wilmington, and then afterward have dinner at a Chinese restaurant located near the campus of the University of North Carolina at Wilmington, more commonly called UNCW. "It is going to be a very special evening. Focus on that!" she ordered herself. But it wasn't easy ignoring her still wildly beating heart.

Chapter Two

Downtown Wilmington
Adjacent to the Cape Fear River

Walking slowly along River Walk, a boardwalk that runs the length of downtown Wilmington adjacent to the Cape Fear River, and breathing in through her nose and out through her mouth, Cathy was still trying to slow her heart rate when a car pulled out of a nearby parking lot and kept pace next to her. She tried not to look at the car. The driver and his passenger were taking pictures. *It's a little late for tourist season,* Cathy thought irritably. *Maybe they're from Canada. We are getting more and more tourists down here during our off-season. They must be trying to get pictures of the battleship. If they'd just wait a minute, they could get the ship and not me.* Turning her head to say something to the passenger with the camera, her mouth flew open and the car sped off. It looked like the same dark sedan that had almost run the two of them over. She tried to read the license plate, but it was covered with mud. With knees that suddenly felt like jelly, she sank down on one of the park benches. *Was that just coincidence? Am I being paranoid?* "Stop it!" she commanded the voice in her head. Rising slowly and shakily, the woman continued walking toward the college.

Cathy had just passed the Henrietta III, the largest riverboat in North Carolina, when her cell phone rang. Thinking that it was John, she gulped noisily and tried to put a smile in her voice: "Hi there."

Peter's deep voice responded from the other end, "Well, hi there to you, too. What a nice greeting."

Cathy couldn't hide the disappointment in her voice: "Oh, hi, Peter. What's up?"

Pretending not to hear the change of tone, the FBI agent continued, "I'm downtown and just spotted your PT Cruiser. How about grabbing some lunch with me?"

"Sorry, I just finished having lunch with Linda. We've been working on the wedding."

"Well then, why don't the two of you meet me for coffee?"

"Linda left and I have plans for this afternoon."

Irritation resonated through the phone: "Don't tell me. Let me guess. With the famous visiting professor." The statement dripped with sarcasm.

"As a matter of fact, yes." Cathy tried hard not to sound defensive.

The next words sounded razor sharp and ice cold: "Am I still invited for Thanksgiving or not?"

Cathy's voice softened: "Of course you are. Linda and David will be here. Since you and I are best man and matron of honor, or since I'm divorced, something between the maid and matron of honor, I thought next weekend would be the perfect time to work out any last-minute details that need attending." Cathy stopped at the end of River Walk. "Look, I've got to get going. I'm sorry about this afternoon, but I'll call you in a few days about Thanksgiving."

Not wanting to argue or, for that matter, hear the hurt in his voice, the instructor flipped her phone shut before Peter could respond. After the episode with the car, she just wasn't up for more confrontations. *Sorry, Peter.*

Walking up the hill toward the college and then pausing at the top, Cathy gritted her teeth. Peter was sitting in his silver Dodge Ram truck right in front of the entrance to Ekim College. *If he is sitting here and not at my school where my car is parked, he must have already known that I am meeting John this afternoon. Why the charade on the phone?* Anger rose now. Her only hope was that he had not gone inside and had words with John. *Peter is getting entirely too possessive. I'll have to put a stop to this once and for all.* Cathy raised her hand to get his attention, but before she could call out, the FBI agent pulled away. *That's just as well; I want to calm down before I say what I have to say.*

The middle-aged instructor crossed the street and was about to reach for the door to the college when it suddenly swung open, revealing a swarthy-complexioned man who tipped his Panama hat in her direction. Cathy's forehead wrinkled in concentration. *He looks familiar.* As he walked away, she wondered aloud, "Now where have I seen him before?" The woman paused in concentration. "Oh, I know. I saw him at John's hotel."

Cathy entered the eerily quiet building that housed Ekim College. While bustling with students during the week, on a Sunday afternoon it was like a tomb. Hating elevators and having a secret fear of being trapped in them, Cathy decided to take the stairs to the second floor. Just as she reached the second-floor landing, the elevator doors opened then closed. She scowled. *Oh, I hope that wasn't John going for coffee. With the amount he drinks, he really should switch to decaf.*

Walking down the hall, the tap-tap-tapping of her heels echoed throughout the deserted corridor. Approaching the physics auditorium and attached lab, Cathy saw no visible light under the double doors. She opened one door just a crack. "John. John? Are you in there?" The only reply was the creaking from the slowly turning blades of an ancient overhead fan. "That must have been him in the elevator." Checking her watch and sighing, Cathy murmured, "I hope he won't be long." Resigned to waiting, she stepped back into the hall and leaned against the wall. After a few moments, she slid down the wall to the floor. "Might as well be comfortable!" She leaned her head back and closed her eyes.

Cathy's eyes popped open and she checked her watch. A half an hour had gone by. *If he doesn't hurry up, we'll miss the play.* Her face suddenly brightened and she snapped her fingers. *Of course, why didn't I think of this before?* Taking out her cell phone to call his, she continued smiling. *I think I'll kid him about being the absent-minded professor.*

Cathy's smile turned to a frown as his cell phone rang and rang. Realizing that the same ringing heard through the phone receiver was also coming from the dark interior of the physics lecture hall, a puzzled look replaced the frown. Cathy knew that John would not forget their date and would have called if something else had come up. She doubted that he would leave his cell phone on the podium in the auditorium. The hair began to prickle on the back of Cathy's neck. Her brain whispered over and over, *Something's wrong. Something's wrong.* Her heart hammered wildly for the third time that day. She again opened the doors to the auditorium and lab, feeling along both walls for the light switch. Finding none, Cathy propped one of the doors open with her purse. While the light from the hall helped with the upper part of the auditorium, it did little to illuminate the lower section that housed the lab and demonstration area.

The now nervous woman walked gingerly down the steps, passing more and more into shadow. Near the bottom, her fingers finally fell on a light switch. Sighing with relief, she flipped the switch and the great hall was bathed in bright light. Turning around, her sigh of relief turned into a scream of terror as there lay John Marley, impaled between his own beds of nails. His now sightless eyes bulged out of their sockets as blood oozed from hundreds of nail wounds. The room swayed and the lights began to spin like a kaleidoscope gone berserk. Suddenly, everything faded to black as the horrified woman crumpled to the ground.

Chapter Three

Cathy's scream reverberated throughout the hallways of the deserted school. A weekend security guard burst through the door with his gun drawn. Seeing a distraught woman slumped over the obviously dead professor, he cautiously eased his way over and pulled her back. Holstering his gun, he forced himself to swallow the bile that had risen in the back of his throat, stepped back to the body, and automatically felt for a pulse. Finding none, he radioed for an ambulance and the police.

Cathy was only vaguely aware of being led out of the room and seated in a chair. Although several minutes had actually passed, to Cathy it seemed like only an instant later that the hallway filled with people. Someone passed something pungent under her nose and she began to cough. "She'll be all right now, lieutenant," a doctor said as he straightened up.

The lieutenant held Cathy's wallet in his hand. "We needed to find out who you were, Ms. Cleveland, but you were in no shape to tell us, so we took the liberty of looking for ourselves."

"That's fine, lieutenant." Someone passed a glass of water to Cathy, which she gratefully accepted. The gurney carrying the bagged body of John Marley rolled by. The pupils of Cathy's eyes dilated and her throat constricted, causing her to choke on the water.

The detective gently patted her on the back and then turned her away from the gurney. "If you would just answer a few questions." Cathy had started to nod her head in the affirmative when Peter Channing burst through the door. "She won't be answering any of your questions, lieutenant." Channing flashed his FBI identification. "This investigation is being taken over by our department."

"Like hell it is!" the lieutenant exploded. "We haven't even established yet that there is anything to investigate. For all we know the professor got sloppy with the placement or height of the nails. This could simply be a tragic accident."

Cathy interrupted, "John was very careful. He double-checked all his equipment before every demonstration."

The lieutenant turned quickly back to the badly shaken woman. "So you knew the professor that well, did you?"

Before Cathy had a chance to answer, the FBI agent stepped between them. He knew that in Cathy's current state of mind she would continue to answer the lieutenant's questions as long as eye contact was maintained. Channing invaded the lieutenant's space and was practically nose-to-nose with him when he barked, "Call your superiors. Either way, this investigation is ours." The agent turned on his heel, grabbed the now totally confused Cathy roughly by the elbow, forced her to stand up, and practically shoved her down the stairs and out of the building.

"You're hurting me," Cathy complained as she tried to wrestle her arm free from Peter's vice-like grip.

"Just get in the truck and then we'll talk." The FBI agent lightened his grip slightly but kept propelling her forward.

Cathy's mind swirled in a jumble of thoughts. *Had John's death really just been a tragic accident?* She remained skeptical. *He was always so careful to check his equipment before he did his demonstrations. And another thing, he had done the bed of nails demonstration a hundred times already; why did he feel he needed to practice it again?* A wave of doubt and fear swept over Cathy. *But if it wasn't an accident, why in the world would anyone want to kill a harmless professor?* Her eyes darted toward Peter. *He had been parked in front of the college. Why?* She tried to slow down, but Peter kept forcing her forward. She would have stumbled and fallen, but Peter's rough handling kept her on her feet and moving.

Reaching the truck, Peter unlocked the passenger door and pushed her inside. "We have to go to headquarters immediately. You need to answer some questions."

Me? Cathy thought as she massaged her now sore arm. *What about you?* Peter jumped in the driver's side, gunned the engine, and they sped off.

Chapter Four

At headquarters, Peter and the college instructor/new agent were ushered into the office of the woman who served as their immediate FBI supervisor, Ms. Emma Grayson. Approximately the same age, but with short gray curls in contrast to Cathy's highlighted layers, the two women had hit it off immediately when Cathy came on board earlier in the fall. Up until now the college instructor had had no actual assignments for the Bureau. It was understood she would work only when her special talents were needed. Cathy had not seen her FBI supervisor in almost a month. Cathy refused the offered chair, so Emma Grayson skipped the usual pleasantries and got right down to business. "What have you gotten yourself into?"

Ignoring the question by her superior, the novice special assignments agent instead asked one of her own. "Why is the FBI interested in John's death? The police think it could have been an accident."

Peter began to answer when Cathy caught the slight shake of his superior's head. The stress of finding John's body in such a ghastly manner and then the rough manhandling at the college and in the truck had taken its toll. Suddenly, the poor woman snapped and yelled almost hysterically, "Why won't you tell me what is really going on here? I can tell you're hiding something. What is it?" A tense silence filled the room. Looking from face to face and willing herself to calm down, she continued, "Well if you won't tell me what's going on, at least tell me why you are taking this out of the local police's hands."

Ms. Grayson came from behind the desk and sat on its front edge. "Look, you are one of us, even if only for special assignments. It's standard procedure to conduct an investigation when one of our own is involved. Makes sense, right?"

The unperturbed demeanor irritated Cathy even more, but she thought about what her supervisor said. It did make sense. Breathing in deeply, and taking the previously offered seat, she listened more agreeably to Ms. Grayson's next question: "Why did you go to Ekim College?"

"I had a date with John Marley and was supposed to meet him in the lab."

"What happened when you arrived?"

"When I got there, I saw that it was dark, so I waited in the hallway."

"About how long did you wait in the hall?"

"About a half an hour."

"Are you sure about the time?"

"Yes. I checked my watch because I didn't want to be late for the performance."

"Then what?"

"I called his cell phone, but when I heard it ringing from the front of the demonstration area, I decided to investigate." Describing the grizzly discovery after turning on the lights, Cathy visibly paled. Peter unobtrusively handed her a bottle of water that she gratefully accepted and sipped, all the while continuing to talk.

"Did you see anyone else near the entrance or in the building?"

It was then that Cathy remembered the man in the Panama hat and related this information.

"Is that everything you remember?"

Cathy was about to shake her head affirmatively but stopped. "I did hear the elevator doors close just as I got to John's floor." She then turned toward Peter and hesitated. *Why isn't Peter saying anything? Should I mention seeing him outside the building when I got there?* She decided to keep quiet until she could confront him herself. "That's really all I can remember."

"I'm going to have you describe the gentleman in the hat to one of our sketch artists and see what the computer can come up with." The FBI supervisor buzzed for her administrative assistant. "Take Ms. Cleveland to Theresa."

After Cathy left the room, Emma Grayson turned to her subordinate. "What do you think?"

Channing looked sharply at his superior. "Think about what?"

Grayson crossed back behind her desk and sat down. "Come on, Peter. Do you think she knows more than she's saying?"

Leaning across the desk, there was an angry edge in Peter's voice. "I told you before, Cathy doesn't know anything. She's one of us, remember?"

The FBI supervisor looked up at the agent and sighed. "Don't let your personal feelings get in the way of your better judgment. You're a professional, so start acting like one and not a naïve, lovesick little boy." Pausing, her tone softened. "I'm sorry to sound so harsh, but it's for your own good."

Before he could respond further, Cathy walked back into the room. Almost simultaneously, Emma Grayson's intercom buzzed. She pressed the button. "What is it?"

"A police Lieutenant Kubecki is here to see Mr. Channing."

The FBI supervisor scowled at her subordinate, who straightened up. "Escort Lieutenant Kubecki in, please."

Entering the room, the lieutenant nodded to the two women before focusing his attention on Channing. "I'll come right to the point. We got a witness that places you near the Ekim College entrance about the time the professor died."

Grayson spoke rapidly: "Are you ruling his death a homicide, lieutenant?"

Lieutenant Kubecki shifted uneasily. "Not yet."

"Then why the questions?"

"I'm just trying to cover my bases."

It was Channing's turn to ask a question: "May I ask who the witness is?"

"Do you admit to being in the area then?"

He shrugged and laughed. "Not necessarily."

The lieutenant's voice took on a menacing quality and his eyes bore into Channing's as he took a step toward him: "Then you deny it."

The agent stepped back and answered more slowly this time: "I didn't say that either."

The accusatory look on Cathy's face confirmed to everyone in the room that she also knew Peter had been there beforehand; however, the penetrating scowl on her supervisor's face warned the new FBI agent to keep her mouth shut.

Exasperated, the lieutenant looked from one member of the group to another. "All right, it was the shop owner across the street from the college. He noticed you sitting in your truck in front of the college just an hour or so before we got the 911 call. Being Sunday, not much goes on, so you just sitting there made him nervous. He took down your license plate number just to be on the safe side."

Emma Grayson turned and glared sharply at the veteran agent, who shifted uncomfortably. "We are in the middle of an ongoing investigation, lieutenant. I was there on official business. I'm afraid that's all I can tell you at the moment," Peter said.

When the lieutenant started to protest, the FBI supervisor quickly confirmed her subordinate's statement. "I'm sorry, lieutenant. All we are at liberty to say at the moment is that it's an ongoing investigation that could very well involve homeland security."

An unhappy lieutenant threw his arms up in exasperation and stomped out of the room. The door hadn't closed completely when Cathy exploded, "What investigation? Why haven't I been told about this?" Looking from grim face to grim face, a warning siren went off inside her brain. "Don't tell me, let me guess. You were investigating me too, weren't you." It was a statement, not a question. Their silence said it all. Shaking her head, she looked directly at Peter. "You keep

Chapter Six

Cathy lived in a lovely three-bedroom redbrick ranch-style home nestled on an acre of land that used to be part of an old nursery. With the building boom in the area, it was probably one of the few truly wooded lots left in New Hanover County. The lot was filled with pines, ornamental cherries, dogwoods, and magnolia trees, as well as azaleas, crepe myrtles, hydrangeas, and camellia bushes. The yard was awash with color almost every season of the year. In the summer, the crepe myrtles bloomed in fuchsia and pink, while the hydrangeas added a hint of purple. During winter the camellias painted the yard with colors of red, pink, candy stripe, and white. When spring arrived, the azaleas provided a breathtaking splash of red, purple, pink, and white underneath the pine trees. In the fall, the hardwood trees' leaves turned the yard rust, yellow, and dark red.

Located just a few miles from Wrightsville Beach, Cathy had originally moved there with seven cats, affectionately named after the seven dwarfs. They were her family. Sadly, now there were only six. Doc, the cat always considered the smartest, had succumbed to cancer earlier in the fall. Cathy's eyes still filled with tears whenever she thought of her precious little companion.

Tonight, getting out of the car to open the gate and looking up, Cathy noticed an especially black sky as passing clouds obscured the

31

stars and the moon. Clutching her jacket tightly about her shoulders and shivering slightly, the still distraught woman got back into the car. She pulled in the dark drive, put the car in park, and gazed at the house. The interior appeared blacker than the night sky. A chill again ran up her spine. Why? She couldn't say. This house had always been a sanctuary from the outside world, but not tonight. Continuing to look around, nothing seemed wrong, and yet? *It's been a horrible day! I'm exhausted. No wonder I'm so jumpy.* Leaving the car and heading for the front door, the woman kept the keys in her right hand with one key protruding between each finger. *Just to be on the safe side!*

The phone was ringing as Cathy entered. Depositing her purse and keys on the dining room table, she dove for it. "Hello."

"C.C., it's Linda. Are you okay? We just heard about John Marley on the evening news."

Hearing the concerned voice of her best friend was too much for the distraught woman. Breaking into sobs that shook her whole body, Cathy blubbered, "Oh, Linda, it was awful. When I found his body…"

The computer analyst broke in. "Wait a minute. You found the body?" There was no response from the other end of the line. "Are you still there?" Linda heard a muffled sob in response. "Go get a glass of water, drink some slowly, take a deep breath, and then come back to the phone and tell me everything that happened from the time I left you in front of the restaurant."

Grateful for her friend's level headedness, Cathy did exactly as told. Returning to her cordless phone, she took it and the glass of water into the living room and sank down on the slouch couch. Only after sipping on the water and gaining control of her emotions did the college instructor proceed to tell her best friend everything, starting with the men in the car taking pictures and ending with her storming out of the FBI office. Linda became so quiet that now it was Cathy's turn to wonder if she was still there.

"Oh, I'm here all right, C.C. But let me call you back in five minutes."

Dejectedly, Cathy hung up and looked around. It was then she noticed that none of the cats had come to greet her. Panic set in as she called their names. Slowly, each one appeared. Two had hidden under the bed, one under the cover on the couch, one on top of the bookcase in the living room, and another in a bathroom cabinet. Finally hearing a plaintiff cry behind the washer, the exhausted woman strained to reach the last one, Dopey. The lanky cat had gotten herself trapped. Liberating the helpless cat from her temporary prison, Cathy hugged Dopey tightly. "But why were you all hiding? You guys only do this when strangers come to the house." Alarm bells went off in her psyche. She straightened up, almost dropping poor Dopey on her head. Cathy's eyes darted from side to side.

Quickly, the new FBI agent ran back out to the car and retrieved a FBI-issued revolver kept locked in the glove compartment of her cherry-red and wood-sided PT Cruiser convertible. Carefully, she reentered the house, cautiously turning on lights in every room. Looking in all the closets and under the beds, she found everything to be in order, yet she couldn't shake this creepy feeling. *And that still doesn't tell me why the cats hid.*

Cathy jumped when the phone rang again. Being careful to put the safety on first, she set the gun down and put the phone on speaker. "C.C., it's me. I just talked to David. We are on our way down." When Cathy tried to protest, Linda cut her off. "Don't argue. I just got off the phone with Emma Grayson, and she's agreed to tell our respective employers up here that we are needed. We'll throw some stuff in a suitcase and be at your house in about two hours."

A grateful Cathy hung up the phone. She put the gun in the cabinet next to her bed and returned to the living room. As each cat vied for a spot on her lap, on the back of the couch, or snuggled on either side, Cathy again thought of John Marley and goose bumps appeared on her arms. She shivered involuntarily. Although the thermostat in the house was set at seventy-two, the woman felt ice-cold. Wrapping up in a blanket, her thoughts turned to Peter and their strained relationship. Not realizing until this moment how much she had come to depend on his quiet strength, an ache began to well up from deep inside. Even though they hadn't seen that much of each other lately, Peter had been the one person she could turn to in time of trouble, but no longer. Replaying the conversation in Emma Grayson's office, anger once again swelled in her chest. *They honestly don't know if they can trust me. I thought we were supposed to be a team.* Her mind raced from thought to thought. *And how in the world could poor John have been involved in any kind of a threat to homeland security? It doesn't make sense.*

The ringing of the phone for the third time brought Cathy out of her reverie. She reached for it. This time it was Peter. As soon as she heard Peter's voice, a wall went up around her emotions and heart. Warily she responded, "What do you want?"

"C. C., we need to talk."

"Unless you are ready to trust me enough to tell me what is going on, we have nothing to talk about."

"You heard Emma. You know I can't, not just yet. But soon. I promise."

Cathy's heart might as well have been in a freezer. "Well, until that time we have nothing more to say to each other. Good-bye."

"I love you, Cathy." A dial tone was all Peter heard in reply. The line was already disconnected.

A Vacant Lot Near Cathy's House

Seated in a van parked in the drive behind the vacant house adjacent to Cathy's, Omar and Carl grinned at each other. Carl had worked with Omar on two other occasions and been the one to recruit him for this job. While Omar was definitely not the brightest bulb in the pack, Carl knew he would follow orders without question. Omar now chuckled aloud. "Hey Carl, do you realize that you and that chick have the same initials, C.C.?" The murderer stared at Omar blankly. "You know, for what people call you, Cutthroat Carl."

Austin sneered. "Yeah, and maybe Ms. Cleveland's C.C. will stand for Cleveland's Cutthroat when I get through with her."

Omar looked questioningly at his partner. "Why? It's obvious that this woman doesn't know anything."

"True, but I may just cut her throat anyway." The killer opened the van's door and stepped into the crisp night air. "Omar, I want you to continue to monitor what is said in the house. Let me know what they talk about. In the meantime, I better let Mr. Wills know what is going on."

When the van door slammed shut behind Austin, Omar stretched and shook his head. "Man, that guy is crazy!"

Chapter Seven

By the time Linda and David arrived, Cathy had a fire burning brightly in the fireplace. The airline pilot enveloped his fiancée's best friend in a bear hug. "Linda filled me in on everything on the drive down. What can we do to help?"

"Did Emma Grayson tell you anything when she cleared you to come here?"

"Nothing. Sorry," Linda apologized.

"Then the first thing you can do to help me is to try to find out what the heck is going on."

David deposited their bags in the guestroom, then returning to the living room, stopped at the minibar and poured a glass of Riesling for each of them. "Count on it. Tomorrow morning, first thing, Linda and I have to report to headquarters anyway. We'll see if we can't straighten this mess out. But right now, let's go over it once more."

Cathy's face clouded over. "I'd really rather not."

"Please," her friend implored. "I'd like David to hear it from you. I might have forgotten something or left something out."

So, again, Cathy recited her woeful tale of that awful day, starting with the men in the car taking her picture and ending with the hidden cats.

The Surveillance Van

A jubilant Omar picked up his cell phone and dialed Carl's number. "Tell Mr. Wills that I think we may just have developed a direct pipeline into FBI headquarters."

Cathy's House

The phone rang. When Cathy didn't reach for it, Linda asked if she should answer it. The woman nodded. "Please. For the last hour it has rung nonstop. Reporters keep calling. Somehow they know I discovered the body. Now they are clamoring for all the gory details. I don't know how they got this number. At first I kept hanging up. Now I don't answer and let the calls go directly to voicemail."

David crossed to the phone. "Let me handle this." He picked up the receiver and listened as still another reporter identified himself and asked for Ms. Cleveland. "Look, Ms. Cleveland's only comment is to say, 'No comment'." He hung up the phone and disconnected it from the wall. The distinguished airline captain looked over at Cathy. "Hope you don't mind."

"Not at all. Mom is spending Thanksgiving with my brother and his family in Phoenix. They have my cell number if she needs to get a hold of me. I only wish I'd had the presence of mind to do that earlier." She got up and stifled a yawn. "I'm exhausted and I feel one of my sinus headaches coming on. If you don't mind, I'm going to take a Benadryl and crawl into bed."

Linda hugged her best friend tightly. "Everything will be all right. I promise!"

Cathy sighed, walked to her bedroom door, and was about to close it. Instead, she turned back around. "Not for John. Never again for John. Goodnight." She sighed again and closed the door.

The engaged couple talked late into the night in the privacy of the guest bedroom.

"What do you think this all means?" asked Linda.

David shrugged. "I have no idea."

"I still can't believe that the FBI suspects her of doing something illegal. That's just insane."

"I'm sure Emma Grayson is just doing her job."

"And what about Peter? Why didn't he say anything before this?"

David felt his loyalty being divided between his fiancée and his best friend. "Remember, he has a job to do, too."

Linda's head snapped up. "I can't believe you're actually defending him!"

The airline pilot rubbed his beloved's shoulders to try to calm her down. "Let's just wait until we talk to him tomorrow. Remember, there are usually two sides to everything." Understanding the strain Linda felt for her friend, David purposely kept his voice low and even.

"Okay, okay." Linda grumbled, but the massage was having its desired effect. Her head and shoulders had just begun to droop when she suddenly snapped back up. "But how do you explain the freaky behavior of Cathy's cats when she got home?"

"Who knows? He stopped rubbing her shoulders, looked sideways at Linda, and smirked. "After all, cats are like women."

Linda glared at her fiancé. "What's that supposed to mean?"

"It means they're moody." David ducked as a pillow flew over his head.

Chapter Eight

d Warehouse
nington International Airport
ning

ung men sat on cold metal chairs around a large
le inside a deserted warehouse near Wilmington's
port. Harold Wills stood in front of them. Dressed
ture charcoal gray suit, but this time with a gray and
ked like someone attending a funeral. This was
d effect. Using his best addressing-the-jury voice,
I want you to know that I share in your grief over the
John Marley. It was a tragic accident. I know that he
ed each of you for this very special Wilmington
he selected others from around the Carolinas for
similar projects in cities like Charleston and Myrtle Beach. Let me
assure you that his dream and yours of humbling the upper classes
did not die with him. I am here to help you honor his memory by
completing that dream next weekend."

The young men looked around the table at each other but said
nothing. Finally, one folded his arms and asked, "How?"

"His plan was absolutely brilliant!" Harold Wills' voice boomed.
"Next Saturday is the annual Wrightsville Beach Holiday Flotilla."

"I heard about the flotilla when I was a child but I never went to
it. What is it exactly?" asked the student with the folded arms.

"It's a holiday parade, only on the Intracoastal Waterway. Boats of every description are decorated and lit up for the holidays. They start at the Wrightsville Beach Bridge, parade down the Intracoastal Waterway, turn into Banks Channel, and finish at the end of Wrightsville Beach."

The young man with the folded arms still looked quizzical. "What has that got to do with us?"

Wills stood appraising this inquisitive young man who seemed to have appointed himself the leader of the group. "What's your name son?"

"Anthony, sir."

"Well, Anthony, Professor Marley arranged for each of you to be entered in the Flotilla. Motorboats and sailboats, along with the appropriate decorations, are currently waiting for you."

Quizzical, confused expressions were now painted on the faces of each young man. Anthony again spoke for the group: "What has participating in the Flotilla got to do with bringing the upper class to their knees?"

"Look around you. Hidden in this warehouse are enough explosives to level half of Wilmington." Some of the young men jumped up in a panic. "Sit down. Sit down." Wills waved his arms to restore order. "They can't go off without a detonator." Those who had jumped up looked around rather sheepishly and again took their seats, somewhat reluctantly. "When you leave today and everyday this week, you will each fill your car with them, placing them in your respective boats. When you are spread out during the flotilla, you will drift the boats close to shore all along the route. At a precise predetermined moment the boats will blow up, taking with them those monstrosities that the rich call homes, which, as we all know, are nothing more than a way for them to laud their wealth over us."

"What about all the innocent people that will die, along with the rich and their fancy homes?" asked another young man named Timothy. "Hundreds of people from all over the region come to watch that parade, not just the rich. I know because my dad used to take me to it when I was little."

Wills leveled his gaze at this new young man. "Casualties of war." Looking around at the rest, he added in his best summation-to-the-jury tone, "And make no mistake, gentlemen, this is a war if we ever hope to even out the inequities between the wealthy and powerful of this country and those of us who have to work hard everyday of our lives."

"I still don't understand how destroying their homes will benefit us?" pressed Timothy.

"It will send a strong message. Before the rich built those ugly monstrosities, you could walk for miles along the shore lines of both the marsh and the ocean."

"You can still walk along the ocean," Timothy persisted.

The attorney now glared openly at the young man as if he were a hostile witness. "That may be true, but the area is no longer pristine. Their egos have built eyesores, ruined the natural habitats of the pelicans and turtles. Because of their selfish ways, those of us who don't have the money for the fancy waterfront properties must content ourselves with looking between their houses at the marshland or finding the few public walkways out to the beach. Is that fair? Is that equal?" A few of the young men nodded in agreement. This was the reaction Wills had counted on. His volume cranked up a notch. "Don't you want to see them punished for their egotistical ways? Wouldn't you once again like the islands to be available for everyone to enjoy?" Now the young men nodded enthusiastically. "There is no other way to get through to their kind. Believe me, less radical things have been tried, but it's no use. They own the politicians." Many of the young men now applauded. Sensing the tide had turned; Timothy stared at the floor and shifted his weight but said nothing more.

"What about us?" still another asked. "How do we escape the inferno?" The rest stopped nodding and the applause died as quickly as it began.

"The timers on the explosives will be preset. At a predetermined time you will slip over the boat's side and swim to the closest dredge island. There you will wait until you are picked up by one of my associates." Wills looked from young man to young man. "Any more questions?"

"Yeah." Anthony raised his hand. "Call me stupid, but with only six boats, won't they take out only maybe one row of houses, if we're lucky, before the New Hanover fire departments race to the rescue and extinguish the flames?"

Smart boy! Wills smiled approvingly at the self-proclaimed leader. "You would be absolutely correct if the area fire departments could reach the houses. But one of the boats will actually be detonated under the bridge leading to the island. With the only access destroyed, just a few fire trucks available, and a little ocean breeze, the inferno should spread quickly. Remember, a lot of the structures are made of wood and built extremely close together. Don't forget all those boats tied up at the docks and in the marinas. Most of them are full of fuel. When those go up, the night sky will be filled with an orange glow visible for miles." There was an uneasy silence. The attorney looked around. "Now I hope that's answered all your questions." Indicating Omar, he concluded, "Then my associate here will see to the explosives and give you your boat assignments. For security reasons, you are not to tell anyone else which boat is yours or where it is currently docked. You are not even to tell each other. Is that understood?" The students nodded. "Good, because we have them scattered throughout several marinas."

Walking out of the warehouse and into the early morning light the attorney turned to his subordinate. "I want you to plant enough explosives on the north end of the dredge island to obliterate half of it. Do that tonight. I don't want any slip ups."

"When that many explosives go up, those guys will be toast."

Wills slowly shifted his gaze toward Carl as if instructing a child: "Of course. My employer wants no witnesses."

Carl Austin gazed back into the warehouse and grinned. "I wonder what those losers would say if they knew that the real brains behind all this was not Professor John Marley but actually a billionaire himself whose only interest is in the real estate."

"Starting with Wrightsville Beach, as each calamity strikes, he will be able to buy the choicest real estate up and down the East Coast for pennies on the dollar," mused Harold Wills.

Taking his knife from its sheath and gazing at its blade, Cutthroat Carl smirked, "The fools who own it now will beg him to take it off their hands."

Wills nodded. "And the beauty of this plan is that this will all be attributed to just another terrorist group attempting to bring this country to its knees." Looking at the knife and the crazy glint in Carl's eyes, Wills shifted uncomfortably. "Put that knife away and go help your friend Omar."

Waiting a few minutes after Carl departed, Wills walked back into the warehouse and crossed to one of the offices. He sat at a large metal desk, opened his briefcase, and took out a thick folder. Placing reading glasses on the end of his nose, he opened it and began to read. The folder contained the dossiers on each of the young men in the warehouse. The lawyer had trusted the instincts of John Marley when it came to picking the likeliest candidates for this immense project. Now with Marley gone, however, he felt he had better refamiliarize himself with each of the students.

Wills stared at the first picture. A young man of medium build with almost blue-black hair, olive skin, and dark brown eyes stared back. The attorney picked up the dossier and began reading the biography. Anthony Joe attended Ekim College. He fit the profile that they had looked for perfectly. His hometown was Wallace, North Carolina, where his father had worked in a textile plant that had closed and moved overseas a few years back. The father's age and lack of education turned out to be insurmountable odds. Unable to find other employment, feeling frustrated and humiliated, the man finally committed suicide. Anthony blamed his father's death on the greed of the plant's owner.

Wills picked up the next dossier. Timothy O'Malley also attended Ekim College. Flaming red hair and sky-blue eyes gazed out from his picture. A sprinkling of freckles covered his cheeks and nose. Timothy O'Malley's case was different. He came from a poor family, but one that emphasized education. While Tim's grades guaranteed him a scholarship, his older brother's did not. Still, his brother also dreamed of going to college. The only way he could afford it was by joining the National Guard. He never dreamed that the country would subsequently go to war and that the National Guard would also be required to go. Tim's brother was in Iraq less than a week when the family had been notified of his death. Tim blamed his brother's death on the government and the choices the poor are often forced to make if they hope to succeed in life.

Two other young men, Bobby and Tom Bristol, were brothers, identical twins to be exact. They had been recruited from a college just south of Wilmington. Both were strapping young men with blonde hair and light blue eyes that reflected their Norwegian heritage. Their father had been a farmer near the coast. Two hurricanes, Bertha and Fran, struck the region in 1996, destroying their farming equipment, barn, and farmhouse. After that, the insurance company raised the premium so high that the family couldn't afford coverage. The next hurricanes, Bonnie and Dennis, did major damage to the farm again. Hurricane Floyd was the knockout punch. With no insurance to pay for the damages and FEMA slow to respond, the family was wiped out, leaving them no choice but to sell the farm to a developer. Multimillion-dollar homes replaced the acres of tobacco and cotton. The money the family received from the sale of the property was barely enough to cover all the debts that had accrued. The boys had grown to hate those around them who could afford such huge houses when their family of six was now forced to live in a 14x70 singlewide trailer.

The next young man's name was Ike Wilkes. The haunted hazel eyes in this picture looked out of proportion to the rest of the gaunt face framed by light brown hair. John Marley had recruited Ike from the college to the north of Wilmington. Ike's mother had a heart condition that required major surgery, a procedure still considered experimental. Because of this, her health insurance would not cover the operation. Since the family did not have the resources to pay for the costly operation, the woman had basically been told to go home and die. Her friends tried to raise money, but it was too little too late. Ike's mother had passed away the previous spring.

The final young man, Jonah James, attended night school in Wilmington, trying to get his GED. With dark curly hair and angry dark eyes, he was a product of the streets, in and out of trouble with the law since the age of nine. Jonah had been busted for just about everything imaginable: drugs, stealing, disturbing the peace, even male prostitution. Blaming anyone but himself for his problems, the young man hated everyone. He was a loner, which, to Wills, was perfect.

Harold Wills slowly closed the folder with the dossiers. His forehead creased in concentration as he made a tent with his fingers. He was satisfied with everyone except Timothy O'Malley. The others were obviously angry young men, full of hate, and people who hate are easily manipulated. Timothy, on the other hand, while obviously angry, did not seem to hate, plus he had brains. The lawyer pushed the reading glasses to the top of his head. *If he thinks too much, that kid just might be able to figure out what is really going on. I am definitely going to have to keep an eye on that boy!!!*

Chapter Nine

Cathy's House
Two Miles from Wrightsville Beach

The engaged couple awoke to the aroma of freshly brewed Kona coffee mingled with that of hot, just-out-of-the-oven cinnamon rolls. After showering in the guest bathroom, they emerged to find their hostess placing the freshly baked rolls on a platter. "I noticed you drove your vintage 1969 Mustang down here, David."

David smiled broadly. "She hasn't been on a long road trip in quite a while, so I figured this was as good a time as any. I wanted to put the top down, but that one wouldn't let me." He pointed an accusing finger at his fiancée.

Sticking her tongue out, Linda crossed her eyes. "Can you imagine going seventy down Interstate 40 in forty-five degree weather?"

Cathy looked apologetically at David. "Actually, no. It may be in the sixties during the day, but it is cold at night."

"I would have cranked the heat up."

"That would have been fine for my feet, but what about my head?"

Sensing the light-hearted banter turning into a storm, Cathy sought to change the subject. "You referred to the car as she?"

Linda reached around Cathy to stick her finger in the gooey icing that had fallen off one of the rolls. "That was my question. David even named the car Baby."

David playfully swatted Linda's now sticky fingers. "Well, that's because she is my baby."

"Makes sense to me." Cathy nodded toward the screened-in porch. "Have a seat out there. It's a lovely morning and the leaves have finally changed color. Being from the North, I still find it strange that the leaves don't change color down here until this late in the year."

Sipping on coffee and eating rolls, the pair admired the dogwood, magnolia, and pine trees. Cocking his head to one side, David asked, "What's that I hear?"

"The waterfall and pond I had put in."

"It's so serene here," sighed Linda. Then looking over at her friend, she grimaced, "I'm sorry." It must seem anything but serene to you right now."

Cathy shook her head but said nothing. Tears spilled out from the corners of her eyes.

Later, after Linda and David left for FBI headquarters, Cathy sat reading the newspaper. The lead story on the front page of the local section was the death of the professor. The title read simply, "Nailed!!!" There, next to John's picture, was one of her being hustled out of the building by Peter. She shuddered violently, threw the paper on the table, and was about to enter the house when a familiar truck rumbled up the drive. "Oh no, I just can't deal with him right now."

Getting out of his truck, Peter spied Cathy through the porch screen and yelled, "I've got to talk to you!"

Cathy placed her hands on her hips. "Are you ready to tell me what's going on?"

"You know I can't do that until I get the go-ahead from headquarters."

"Then as I said to you last night, we have nothing more to say to one another." The woman re-entered the house, shutting the sliding glass door that separated the porch from the house. Frustrated, there was nothing more for the agent to do but get back in his vehicle. His wheels spun gravel as he gunned the engine and backed down the drive.

The Surveillance Van

Omar and Carl watched from the back of the van as the truck backed out of the yard. Carl once again removed his knife from its sheath. "I would so like to cut that guy's throat."

Omar moved as far away from his accomplice as possible in such cramped quarters. "You know what Mr. Wills said about killing Channing."

The gleam in Carl's eyes and his next words sent a chill through the ex-con. "Yeah, well, maybe someday it will be Mr. Wills' turn." Then, as abruptly as the gleam entered the killer's eyes, it faded. He looked at his watch. "Hey, I'm starved. There's a Java Joe's just down the street. I think I'll get myself a muffin. You want anything?"

"Yeah. Why don't you bring me back a bagel."

Carl got out of the van and into his black SUV. "I'll be back in a couple of minutes."

"Take your time" was Omar's only reply. What Carl didn't know was that once money had been discussed, the ex-con's primary allegiance instantly switched from Carl to Harold Wills. As soon as the car was out of sight, Omar made a call: "Mr. Wills, I think you should know what Carl just said…"

Chapter Ten

Cathy's College
Downtown Wilmington

Cathy cleaned up from breakfast, fed the cats, showered, and headed for school. She taught at the local community college and had two classes to teach that morning: Introduction to Communication and Interpersonal Communication.

When both classes were finished, Cathy headed for her office. The college instructor felt as if she had just gone through the motions of teaching instead of being the dynamic instructor that she was, the one who had been voted the college's instructor of the year the previous year. *The way I feel right now, Interpersonal Communication should be called Impersonal Communication! I feel as if my brain is encased in cotton. I just can't concentrate. It sure doesn't help when coworkers stop me in the hall to express their condolences or, worse yet, want the morbid details of finding his body.*

The middle-aged instructor reached her office and closed the door part way, not enough to be thought gone, but just enough so as not to be seen. Cathy wanted no more expressions of sympathy and no more questions.

Her required office hours were dragging by when the phone rang. Sighing heavily, she picked up the receiver: "Cathy Cleveland, may I help you?"

"Cathy, it's Linda. Can you meet us at home? We have news."

"I'm on my way." She hung up the phone, grabbed her jacket and headed for the door.

The now lively instructor stopped by her department head's office to tell him that she was leaving. He was on the phone and simply waved her off. Briefly placing a hand on the speaker portion of the receiver, he yelled, "I just got a call. I know you've got to go." With those words, her boss returned to his phone call and she practically ran to the exit that led to the parking lot.

Cathy's House

Linda paced back and forth in the living room. Looking from Peter to David, she asked, "What do you think this all means?"

Peter shook his head as they heard the crunch of tires on the gravel drive. "I honestly have no idea."

When Cathy entered the house, the veteran agent jumped to his feet. "Cathy" was all that came out of his mouth before he saw her visibly stiffen at the sight of him.

Lightly touching his arm, Linda said, "Let me." Leading Cathy to the rocker, the part-time FBI agent instructed her best friend to sit down. "You know that composite sketch that was done from the description you gave yesterday?" Cathy nodded. "Well, the computer came up with a name to match that face. Carl Austin."

David cut in. "He's also known as Cutthroat Carl. He likes to cut people for pure pleasure."

Peter took a step toward her. "The point is we don't know who hired him or why that person would want him to take out your friend. Do you?"

"But they were friends," sputtered a confused Cathy.

The other three leaned forward. Linda asked, "Who were friends? What do you mean?"

"This Carl Austin and John were friends."

David crossed the room and sat at Cathy's feet. Staring up into the woman's face, he asked, "What makes you think they were friends?"

Cathy looked down at David. "Because he told me." She looked at the bewildered expressions on the faces of those around her. "One night about two weeks ago, it was very late. I went over to John's hotel room to retrieve a sweater that I had accidentally left there earlier in the evening. I remember I went back because I wanted to wear it the next day. Anyway, I had just gotten off the elevator when I saw that same man leave John's room and head for the parking garage. When I asked John who he was, John told me he was a friend from back home who just happened to be in town, too."

Peter took a step toward Cathy. "Why didn't you mention this before?"

A defiant Cathy jumped up. "I just didn't, all right." She paused. "Look, I'm sorry. I guess I was in shock yesterday."

Peter gently pushed Cathy back into the rocker and, in a quieter tone, asked, "This is very important. Did that man see you that night?"

Cathy thought for a minute. "I don't think so."

Peter exhaled slowly. "Are you sure?"

"I'm not sure, but why would it matter even if he did?"

"Because if he had seen you, then he would know that you are someone who could link him directly to the professor."

Linda tugged on the turquoise scarf tied around her neck. "And that would put her in danger."

"I'm afraid so."

Standing up again and crossing to the fireplace mantle, Cathy reached out and lovingly touched the picture of her mother and deceased father. Finally, she turned and looked at the three people in front of her. "You still haven't told me why the FBI was investigating John."

Peter walked over to the minibar, opened a bottle of water, and took a long drink. Replacing the cap, he began, "While John Marley was lecturing in South Carolina, a male student came to us. He said there was a guest professor on campus that was trying to befriend some of the more disgruntled students, he being one of them. Apparently your friend Marley was asking them a lot of questions."

"What's wrong with that?"

"Nothing's wrong with that on the surface. Except that the questions were things like, 'Are you happy with the way things are in this country? Do you feel like the wealth in this country is unfairly distributed?' Questions that, after 911, made this student nervous enough to come to us."

Cathy laughed incredulously. "Those questions might simply have been John's way of trying to connect with and stimulate a discussion with some students who looked like they needed a mentor. Did you ever think of that?"

Peter's face took on a grave expression. "The FBI did think of that. But, after doing a little digging, they discovered a pattern. The man did the same thing at every campus he went to."

"All campuses have disgruntled students. I still say that maybe John just wanted to help those students."

Linda stepped in between the two, pushing them apart slightly with the palms of her hands. "Your friend asked the same questions at each campus. You've got to admit that's a little weird."

"Weird, maybe yes. But enough for the FBI and Homeland Security to get involved, no." Cathy just could not accept that John was anything but that sweet, slightly crazy professor that she had come to know and admire.

David observed the impasse. "Look, I think what we need is a little time to digest this information. Let's take a break, grab something to eat, and then continue."

Putting her arm around her fiancé's waist, Linda quickly chimed in, "Good idea."

The Surveillance Van

As the four drove off in search of food, Omar hastily dialed the phone. "Mr. Wills, that Cleveland woman saw Austin with the professor at the hotel and also outside the college the day Marley was eliminated. She can directly connect the two of them."

After a moment of silence, the lawyer sighed, "Then Ms. Cleveland will definitely have to be eliminated. Have Carl see to it."

Chapter Eleven

The Estate of Franklin Morse
A Little North of Hampstead, North Carolina
Monday Afternoon

Harold Wills replaced the receiver of the telephone and slowly walked out to his charcoal Mercedes, shoulders slightly slumped and feet shuffling. He dreaded the trip he was about to make. Franklin Morse, head of Morse Industries and one of the ten wealthiest men in America would not be happy, not happy in the least.

Driving north on Highway 17, Wills tried to think of a way to explain to Mr. Morse why things seemed to be unraveling. There was just no easy way to do it. Reluctantly, he turned his car onto a winding drive that curved through a thick pine forest. He couldn't see it, but he knew the forest hid a security system that the White House would envy.

Leaving the forest abruptly behind, the drive ended before a majestic two-story house designed to look, from the front, like "Tara" from *Gone with the Wind*, complete with columns that stretched from roof to veranda. Beyond the house lay the Intracoastal Waterway, and beyond that, the Atlantic Ocean. The midday sun glistening off the water was almost blinding.

Marcus, head of security for Morse Industries, greeted the attorney at the door. Wills didn't know Marcus's last name, but knew some of the man's history. He had been a member of an elite-fighting unit in Iraq when a car bomb ended his dream of making the military his life. Unfortunately, there are not many jobs in the civilian world for trained killers, so when Franklin Morse offered him the position as head of security, Marcus had jumped at it. As Harold Wills straightened his tie, Marcus silently led him into Franklin Morse's study and positioned himself next to the door.

Seated behind an enormous mahogany desk sat a man of medium build but with a formidable aura about him. A confirmed bachelor, his wealth and slightly dangerous mystique kept him in demand with many of the single and even some of the married socialites in both Wilmington and Washington. Dressed in a black turtleneck and red v-necked cashmere sweater, Franklin Morse looked up from the file he was reading only when Wills was standing directly in front of him. "Well, Harold, this had better be important. I had to cancel my weekly golf game because of your message."

"Believe me sir, it is."

Rising and crossing to a giant aquarium, Morse picked up a bottle of fish pellets and fed the assorted tropical fish before asking over his shoulder, "Well then, what is it?"

Wills looked uncertainly at Marcus. Noticing the lawyer's reluctance to talk in front of the security chief, the industrialist ordered Marcus out of the room with a simple nod. Finally, when Marcus had exited and closed the door, Wills started. "You know that we had to eliminate the professor because the FBI was nosing around."

"We were finished with him anyway. So?"

The attorney shifted uncomfortably. "It has just come to my attention that the FBI has been investigating him for some time, actually, a lot longer than we thought."

Franklin Morse crossed back to his over-stuffed desk chair and sat down, waving the obviously distraught man into a seat directly across from him. "Explain."

"Apparently the professor's been under investigation since South Carolina. It turns out a student he tried to recruit there and not this Cleveland woman's ex-boyfriend alerted the authorities."

Morse leaned back in his chair, blinked rapidly, picked up a pencil and began to tap on the desktop. "Does the FBI know anything?"

"No."

"Are you quite sure?" Franklin Morse now leaned forward, carefully returning the pencil to its brown leather holder and placing the palms of his hands flat on the desk. His gaze was so intense Harold Wills felt as if the man's eyes were laser beams capable of passing right through him.

The lawyer again played with his tie. "Yes, sir. Quite sure."

Picking up a pen this time, Morse again began tapping on the desk. "Are we still on track for Saturday?"

The subordinate straightened in his chair. "Absolutely, sir."

Morse's eyes took on a faraway look as his gaze shifted to some imaginary speck on the opposite wall. "Nothing must stand in the way of my acquiring that land. My plans are all in place. Wrightsville Beach will become the mid-Atlantic Miami Beach. There will be nothing but condominiums anywhere you turn. Clearing his throat, he looked back at Wills. "Now, if there is nothing else . . ." Franklin Morse was about to wave him away when Wills cleared his own throat.

"There is another problem, sir. It seems the Cleveland woman can place Carl Austin at John Marley's hotel room a few weeks ago as well as in front of the college the day he was killed."

Mr. Morse jumped up, nearly knocking over his chair. "Get rid of her," he roared.

Wills rose quickly. "It's already being taken care of."

Franklin Morse strode across the room to stare out the window at the Intracoastal Waterway, clasping his hands behind his back. The sight seemed to calm him instantly, "Good."

Walking to the door, the lawyer stopped and turned. "What about Carl Austin?"

Never turning from the window, Morse muttered, "He's become a liability. Get rid of him too."

Harold Wills' Charcoal Mercedes

Once again driving back through the pine forest, Harold Wills uncharacteristically loosened his tie before punching in the number to the surveillance van on his cell phone. The ex-con picked up on the second ring. "Omar, after this is all over, I've got another job for you."

The ex-con grinned. "Gotcha!"

Chapter Fourteen

Cathy's House
Two Miles from Wrightsville Beach
Tuesday Morning

The betrothed couple again arose to the aroma of Kona coffee. This time, however, when they walked onto the screened-in porch, a box of donuts sat on the glass-topped table. "Hope you don't mind," said Cathy, "but I just love them."

"Not in the least," grinned David, as he happily rubbed his hands together in anticipation.

Linda groaned, "You know they'll go straight to my hips." A slow smile then spread across her lips. "I've got to admit that I like them, too."

They were on their second cups of coffee when Peter pulled in. Cathy reluctantly offered him coffee and a donut, which he gratefully accepted. "I got a call just before I left the house. They want you to come down to the office today. They'd like you to give them names or descriptions of any students that John Marley may have been particularly friendly with. We took some pictures while he was under surveillance. They're hoping you can identify a few of them."

"I might be able to identify the ones from my college, but I'll only be able to give you general descriptions of the others."

"At least that will give us a place to start."

"It will have to be this afternoon though. I've got three classes this morning." Cathy looked at her watch and continued, "Wow, I better get a move on." Looking at the other three she asked, "What's on your agenda today?"

Linda answered as the others took their cups and plates to the dishwasher. "We're going to nose around Ekim College this morning. How about meeting us for lunch at Reva's after your classes?"

Cathy eagerly accepted. Despite everything going on, Reva's was one of her favorite places to eat.

After Cathy left, the other three sat down in her living room. Linda started. "What do you really think, Peter?"

"Honestly? I think Cathy is in danger and needs watching. Luckily, because of the Thanksgiving holiday, after today's classes there are none for the rest of the week, so you two can stay with her tomorrow. We'll all be together for Thanksgiving, so that takes care of Thursday."

"What about Friday?" asked David.

Linda raised her hand as if in school. "That's already taken care of. Cathy and I have appointments to see about our gowns, the cake, and the flowers for the wedding."

Peter looked embarrassed. "With all that's happened I'd almost forgotten about your wedding."

David slapped him on the shoulder. "Don't worry about it. But are you still going to be available Friday to get fitted for your tux?" Although the two men had only met in Florida in the summer, the danger they had faced together coupled with the extraordinary courage displayed by both men had made them fast friends. David loved Peter like a brother and wanted no one else to be his best man.

"Absolutely! Now let's get out of here and see what we can find out."

The Surveillance Van

As soon as the three drove off, Omar turned to Carl. "You better let Mr. Wills know their plans. If they get their hands on any of those students, this whole operation could be in jeopardy."

Carl picked up the phone and dialed. After a lengthy conversation, he replaced the receiver.

"What did he say?"

"It's still a go for the Flotilla on Saturday, but we're going to speed up putting the explosives in the boats. Today will be it. After that I'm to take the boys back to the warehouse and keep them there until Saturday."

"What about Cleveland? You never did tell me how you intend to handle her?"

Carl's lips parted in the all-too-familiar malevolent grin exposing those perfectly straight white teeth. "I wouldn't want the dear woman to miss the show on Saturday. In fact I thought I'd give her a ringside seat."

"You're not going to slit her throat?" asked an incredulous Omar.

"I was, but I like this idea better. You see, I thought I'd let Channing see her go up in flames."

Omar frowned. "How are you going to get to her? She's going to be watched constantly now."

Carl shrugged. "Knowing their plans gave me the answer. She is alone right now. I'll grab her as she leaves campus for lunch today." The killer yawned and stretched. "Just thinking about killing always makes me hungry. I'm going to get some fajitas for an early lunch at that Mexican restaurant near here before I round up the boys, take them to the warehouse, then head over to the campus. You want to go grab something?"

Omar shuddered at Carl's nonchalance about it all and declined. "I'm not hungry yet. I'll get something later. But you still haven't said what you are going to do with the lady for three days?"

"No problem. I figured I keep her at the warehouse too."

After Austin left, Omar got out of the van and walked around to stretch his cramped leg muscles. Carl would have to be caught in the inferno along with Cathy Cleveland. The ex-con nodded approvingly. He wasn't really into doing any actual killing, but he'd do what had to be done. Besides, Mr. Wills convinced him that Carl was like a rabid dog that deserved to die. Maybe after this job was done, he would move to a little island somewhere filled with beautiful women. After all, Mr. Wills promised him Carl's share along with his own once it was all over.

Omar smacked his lips and clasped his hands behind his head at just the thought of it. *Yes, a man could live very comfortably on that for a while.*

Chapter Fifteen

Cathy's College
Downtown Wilmington

When Cathy finished teaching her last class for the day, she gathered up the books and papers, placing them in a fake-leather brief case. Leaving the classroom and walking down the hall toward the exit, she still felt caught in the middle of a nightmare. Once outside, even the brisk autumn air couldn't penetrate her consciousness. Her mind, so filled with the events of the last two days, did not register the man walking toward her in the parking lot until he called her name. Looking up to see the familiar Panama hat and white suit, Cathy tried to take a step backwards but stumbled and would have fallen had the man not caught her. "Careful, Ms. Cleveland, I wouldn't want you to hurt yourself just yet." Carl Austin snickered as he pressed a dagger into his captive's side. Keeping a firm grip on the college instructor's arm and a slight pressure on the dagger, the killer propelled the frightened woman forward. "Now we're just going to walk slowly over to that SUV." With a nod, he indicated a black SUV with heavily tinted windows in the far corner of the lot.

The pair had just crossed to the middle of the parking lot when Peter stepped out from behind a parked car, his gun drawn, "Drop the knife, Austin." Carl's attention momentarily shifted to Peter, so the novice FBI agent sprang into action. She jabbed him in the ribs, closely followed by a knee to the groin. Doubling over in pain, the killer loosened his grasp. Cathy wrenched her arm free and ran toward Peter. With the Cleveland woman between himself and Channing, Austin grabbed the opportunity and sprinted for the entrance to the Cotton Exchange, a huge old cotton market that had been converted into unique shops. By the time Cathy finally cleared the line of fire, a crowd was exiting the Cotton Exchange entrance. The veteran FBI agent had no chance to fire his gun. Peter ran to the entrance, but Carl Austin was long gone. "Damn!" Swinging around, he lashed out at the woman he loved and swore to protect. "Why did you run directly toward me? Why didn't you dive for cover? I would have had a clear shot! Have you forgotten all your training?"

Throwing herself into his arms, "Oh, Peter," was all Cathy could manage between sobs.

Peter held the crying woman for several minutes, not saying a word. Finally, pushing away until she was at arm's length, he looked deep into her eyes and shook her lightly. "You are not to go anywhere alone. Do you understand?" Staring at the ground like a child being reprimanded by a parent, she simply shook her head yes. Peter's tone softened. "Look, I'm sorry I yelled. I guess seeing that guy with a knife pressed against your ribs unnerved me. If anything ever happened to you..." Peter didn't finish his sentence; instead he opened his cell phone and called David at the restaurant. The FBI agent briefly explained what had happened, assured David that they both were fine, and told him to go ahead and eat. Closing his phone, Peter turned to a now more composed Cathy. "Feel like walking a little?" Again she just shook her head.

The two left the parking lot and headed toward the Cape Fear River, neither saying a word. As the duo walked along River Walk, Cathy finally managed a meek "Thank you." Again they walked in silence, gazing at the river, the boats cruising up and down it, and the other people out for an afternoon stroll. After about ten minutes, Cathy timidly asked, "How did you know he would try today?"

The pair stopped and sat on one of the benches that overlooked the water. "The truth is I didn't. But I swore to myself last night that I would protect you in spite of yourself." A shadow of a smile played across Cathy's lips before he continued, "It didn't take a genius to realize that you would be most vulnerable in the parking lot, so I told David and Linda to meet us at the restaurant, and I came to find you."

"It's sure lucky for me that you did." Looking up fondly at him now, Cathy reflected on the past. "This certainly isn't the first time you have saved my life. It must be getting pretty old."

Smiling crookedly, the handsome FBI agent placed his hand under her chin and said, "Nah, yours is a life worth saving, even if it over and over again." Looking around, he realized people were starting to watch them. He awkwardly removed his hand from under her chin and pulled her up. "Come on, we better get to the restaurant. I'm starved and I'm sure Linda and David will want to hear all about this latest mishap."

Reva's-on-the-River

Despite everything that had happened, lunch turned out to be a fairly nice affair. After discussing the parking lot episode, the four just sat and let themselves be mesmerized by the river. Finally, it was Peter who broke the spell. "We better get to the Bureau so Cathy can try to identify some of the students recruited by Marley."

An undercurrent of tension suddenly disrupted the peaceful atmosphere. Reluctantly, the group stood up. "Cathy, we'll drop you and Peter off to get your car. Then we'll meet you in the office," David said. This time Cathy didn't argue.

Chapter Sixteen

Cutthroat Carl slammed open the sliding van door in a murderous rage. "That bitch set me up!"

Omar swung around so quickly that he had to grab the table that supported the surveillance equipment to keep his chair from toppling over. "What happened?"

"Channing was waiting and would have killed me, too, if that broad hadn't been stupid enough to run straight for him instead of getting out of the way."

"What are you going to do now?" Omar was almost afraid to hear the answer.

The killer paced back and forth, not saying a word for several minutes. Suddenly, his all too familiar malevolent smile replaced the scowl. He snapped his fingers. "I've got it. Friday, when the bitch and that Tate woman are having their gown fittings, I'll snatch Cleveland right out of the dressing room. That's one place she'll be alone."

"Can we afford to wait that long?"

"No problem. I rounded up all the boys. They are safe and secure in the warehouse."

"Won't they get restless and want to leave? After all, Saturday is a long ways away."

"They have books and magazines to read, video games to play, and movies to watch. Mr. Wills had a pool table and a couple of pinball machines brought in. He even promised them a complete Thanksgiving dinner with all the trimmings." Carl sneered at the thought of that.

"So nothing's changed?" Omar continued eyeing Carl suspiciously.

"Well, there is one thing." Now Carl's maniacal grin covered his entire face, and a totally insane gleam again emanated from his eyes. "Channing is still going to see his lady go up in flames on Saturday, but afterward I intend to slit his throat very slowly."

"But Mr. Wills was very explicit about that. You are not supposed to touch Channing."

Carl turned very slowly and faced Omar. "And who is going to stop me? Harold Wills, with his manicured nails and perfect suit, is too spineless. That just leaves you." Carl slowly crossed to within inches of Omar's face. "You wouldn't consider double-crossing me now would you?"

Omar cowered in his seat. "Me? Of course not!" The ex-con giggled nervously. "Come on now, we're partners."

Carl Austin stepped back and sized up Omar. "Just remember, I'm the one that got you this gig. Before I came along you were just another small-time weasel, in and out of prison. But weasels that piss me off tend to turn into road kill." He waited while the words sank in, watching the pupils of Omar's eyes grow wide with alarm. "Am I clear?"

The ex-con swallowed noisily. "Sure, Carl, sure!"

"Good."

Chapter Seventeen

FBI Headquarters
Downtown Wilmington

Going through the photos was grueling and embarrassing for Cathy. Not only were there pictures of John Marley and his students, but also the college instructor herself had been photographed several times while in the professor's company, including once when exiting his hotel room. Almost reluctantly she looked first at Emma Grayson, then at Peter Channing. "Looking at these pictures, I realize now what it must have looked like to you all." To Peter she spoke barely above a whisper, "I am sorry."

It took the rest of the afternoon to identify what pictures Cathy could and to describe other young men that she had seen with John Marley. By the time the four left the office, the sun had long ago disappeared and had been replaced by a silvery half-moon.

Chapter Eighteen

The Study of Franklin Morse
North of Hampstead
Tuesday Evening

Franklin Morse sat behind the large mahogany desk drumming his fingers. He had not become one of the most powerful men in America by leaving things to chance or fate. His attention to detail in the legitimate world of business was well known. He was no less detail oriented in his not-so-legitimate world as well. The head of Morse Industries did not like what had transpired over the last few days and was beginning to have doubts about Harold Wills as well. His concern was not something to be taken lightly. Silently he pushed a button under his desk. Marcus entered and stood at the door. "You rang for me, sir?"

"Yes. You know the boats that Wills arranged for Saturday? I want you to get exact duplicates." The billionaire industrialist handed Marcus a slip of paper. "Here's where I want you to store them." Marcus read the paper then handed it back to his employer, who placed the paper in the shredder. In seconds it turned to confetti.

Chapter Nineteen

Ekim College
Downtown Wilmington

After a light dinner at a downtown sidewalk café, Linda, David, Cathy, and Peter walked toward Ekim College. The public information office of the college had hastily put together a memorial service for the visiting professor. President Mathias felt it only fitting since John had died there. The actual body would be shipped to a distant relative in Iowa for burial once the authorities were through with it.

As the four entered the lecture hall where the service was to take place, many of Cathy's colleagues, knowing that she and John had been especially close, came up to express their regrets. It was awkward for her with Peter standing so close by, but the FBI agent smiled politely and nodded reassuringly.

During the actual service, Peter, Linda, and David stood in the back of the now packed room. Cathy sat in a special section reserved for the faculties of the various area colleges where John had guest lectured. Her mind was full of so many thoughts and images, some of which she tried unsuccessfully to block out. The middle-aged instructor thought it macabre that the service was being held in the very room in which John died and where she had discovered his hideous corpse, but President Mathias had insisted that it was appropriate and fitting. Every time she glanced in the direction of the minister who was now delivering the eulogy, she shuddered. He stood in the exact spot where the bed of nails containing John's lifeless body had stood.

Cathy decided to focus on the saddened faces around her. John may have done many things wrong, but the one thing he did right was his teaching. The woman's eyes filled with tears. *John, you touched so many lives in such a positive way; why couldn't you be satisfied with that?*

Brushing away the tears and continuing to study the surrounding faces, her reflections of John were interrupted by a realization that made her frown. As soon as the service ended, she hurried to where her friends waited.

Walking down the stairs, Linda took her friend's arm. "Are you all right? That had to be rough, being back in that room, I mean."

"It was, but I'll survive."

When they got to the parking lot, David suggested the group go for a drink. Linda thought stopping somewhere was a good idea, but knowing her best friend's preference asked, "How about stopping at Boombalatti's Homemade Ice Cream for a sundae instead? I happen to know that Cathy is wild about their homemade chocolate-marshmallow ice cream."

Boombalatti's Ice Cream

The ride to Boombalatti's at the Plaza East Shopping Center was silent, but once they were seated, Peter turned to Cathy. "You have had a puzzled expression on your face ever since we left Ekim College. What's going on it that head of yours?"

Licking her chocolate-marshmallow ice cream cone, Cathy looked at the three of them. "Nothing really. I just thought it was kind of freaky that none of the young men in the pictures I looked at today were at the funeral. That's all."

Peter sat up. "None of them were there? Are you sure?"

"Uh huh."

"I'll be back in a minute." The veteran agent excused himself and walked outside.

Linda looked at David. "What was that all about?"

David shrugged. "Beats me."

Three faces stared up at Peter when he returned a few moments later. David quizzed Peter, "What's going on?"

The agent slid back into his chair and returned to his hot fudge sundae. "I just thought Emma should know what Cathy observed at the memorial service."

Chapter Twenty

Cathy's House
Two Miles from Wrightsville Beach
Wednesday Morning

This morning it was Cathy's turn to awake to the smell of her favorite coffee. She brushed her teeth, put on a robe, and opened the bedroom door, only to find David and Peter bustling about the kitchen. "Good morning sleepy head," said a smiling Linda as she set the glass-top table on the porch.

"What's all this?"

"You were so exhausted when we came home last night that the three of us decided to let you sleep in."

Peter stuck his head around the corner. "I invited myself for breakfast. Hope you don't mind."

Cathy smiled. "After saving my life for the second time, how in the world could I possibly mind?"

"David is whipping up his divine cheese and broccoli omelets. Peter's in charge of the blueberry muffins and bacon. I'm pouring the coffee, the orange-mango juice, and setting the table," explained Linda.

"What can I do?"

"You, my dear, should just sit down and enjoy it. We even brought the paper in for you." Linda pointed to the newspaper lying on the table.

Cathy did as she was told. Unfolding the *Wilmington Star-News,* she began to scan the headlines. When she got to the local section, a look of horror crossed her face.

"What is it?" demanded a concerned Linda.

With trembling hands, the woman laid the paper on the table and pointed to the picture of a young man. The headline read, "Partial remains discovered on shore at Carolina Beach." Carolina Beach was just south of Wilmington. "Oh, I saw that when I read the paper earlier. The authorities think he must have been surfing and drowned. What was left of the poor kid, which, from what I gather, wasn't much, apparently washed up on shore. The creatures of the deep had a feast. The only way the authorities were able to identify him was through a DNA match."

"Linda, you don't understand." Cathy pointed again to the picture. "His face was one of those in the photos I looked at yesterday. He was one of the students that John Marley connected with."

Linda grabbed the paper to get a better look at the photo. "You're right. I don't know why I didn't make the connection before."

Peter and David entered with the food. As they all sat down to eat, David asked, "What's going on?"

After Cathy explained, David shrugged. "Could just be a coincidence."

Cathy made a face. "I don't believe in coincidences. And another thing—was he wearing a wetsuit when they found him?"

Linda shifted uncomfortably. "The paper didn't say. Why do you ask?"

"Well, if he wasn't, don't you think it's a little late in the year to be surfing without one?"

Peter wiped his mouth with his napkin, picked up the paper, and scanned the article. "You're right, Cathy. All the surfers I've seen lately are wearing wetsuits. Let me call headquarters and see what I can find out." Taking his cell phone from his pocket, Peter excused himself and walked into the living room.

* * *

The other three had finished eating and had already cleared the table when Peter finally hung up and entered the kitchen. "You were on the phone for quite a while. What's up?" asked David, placing the last dirty dish in the dishwasher.

"Let's all go into the living room and sit down; then I'll fill you in."

Linda refilled her coffee cup and asked if anyone else wanted any. The rest declined, but David smiled. "Careful, sweetheart, since you have cut down on the amount of food you eat, you are drinking more and more caffeine. That is your fourth cup of coffee this morning."

Linda stuck her tongue out. "I have to have some vices or else you wouldn't have anything to bug me about. Besides, the latest studies indicate that coffee may actually be beneficial to a woman's health!"

The airline pilot threw his hands up in mock resignation. "Okay, okay, I surrender. I'm sorry."

The engaged couple settled in on the couch while Cathy sat in the rocker. They all looked up expectantly at Peter, who stood in the middle of the room. "Well?" prompted David.

"The answer to the question about the wet suit is no. He was not wearing one."

Tension began to build. Linda instinctively reached over and took her betrothed's hand. "What does the bureau think?"

"Knowing his connection with John Marley, they believe he was deliberately killed."

Frown lines furrowed the forehead of David's face. "But why?"

Peter shrugged. "Who knows? Maybe he saw something he shouldn't have. Perhaps he wanted out of whatever was going on, or it could have been payback for something he'd done or hadn't done. There are a hundred possibilities."

Tilting her head and watching Peter closely, Cathy finally spoke: "There's something else, isn't there? I can tell. What is it?"

The FBI agent sighed. "You all need to know. I got some more disturbing news while I was on the phone. All those students Cathy identified or described yesterday…"

Cathy nodded slowly. "What about them?"

"They are missing."

"What?" David jumped up, nearly spilling Linda's coffee all over the floor.

"Missing? Are you sure?" Linda's eyebrows rose to a high arch as she carefully set her coffee cup on the end table next to the couch.

"I'm afraid so. After I told Emma that the students weren't at the memorial service yesterday, the Bureau got their addresses and went to pick them up last night. None were home, so our guys waited all night. The students never showed up, and their families, roommates, and sweethearts claim to have no idea where the boys have gone."

"Do you believe that?" Linda's skepticism showed.

"Apparently the bureau does."

"What do you think it all means?" quizzed David, looking into Peter's eyes.

"It could mean they're about to strike. It could mean they know we are on to them. I'm honestly not sure."

"Let's just hope more bodies don't start washing up along the shore." Linda shuddered violently. Her fiancé placed a protective arm around her.

Peter shook his head. "Somehow, I don't think so." Peter crouched down next to Cathy's rocker and placed his hand on its arm. "I do know one thing. It means you are not leaving my sight."

Chapter Twenty-One

The Study of Franklin Morse
North of Hampstead

Harold Wills cowered behind the tan leather chair in Franklin Morse's study. With tie askew and the normally freshly pressed shirt wrinkled and stained with sweat under its arms, the attorney's immaculate appearance had vanished.

"You assured me that body would never be found," hissed a furious Morse.

"Carl Austin disposed of the body. He promised me that kid would disappear forever. Believe me; I was as shocked as you when I read today's paper."

"Austin takes orders from you, just like you take orders from me. He is under your command. If he doesn't do what you say, get rid of him. I told you before that he had become a liability. Why is he still breathing?"

"He will be dealt with, believe me. I have already made the arrangements, but I need him for Saturday."

"Very well, but after Saturday he is to be disposed of. Is that perfectly clear?"

"Yes sir, perfectly clear." Wills made a futile attempt to straighten his tie.

"What about the rest of the young men? Are they secure?"

"We have them sequestered in the warehouse. No one can get to them, I promise you."

"Just see to it. There can be no more slip-ups! Come with me!" commanded Morse as he strode purposefully across the room to the door.

Wills trailed after the industrialist like an obedient dog following his master. The two men crossed the tiled foyer into a room that was bare except for a large marble table in the center. The table actually took up almost the entire room. On it were massive architectural models. One area was labeled Wrightsville Beach, another section read historic district of Charleston, and still a third was titled Myrtle Beach Grand Strand. Each one was covered with high-rise apartments and condos.

Just gazing at these models brought a satisfied smile to the lips of the business giant. "Do you see all this?" Morse indicated the models with a sweeping gesture of his hand. "By Christmas, I will own all the land that these buildings will one day sit on." Pointing to the area of Wrightsville Beach, the man almost purred. "This will become Morse Beach." Indicating the historic district of Charleston, he proclaimed, "I'm going to name this area Franklin Place." Tapping his chin with his fingers, the billionaire industrialist looked at the section entitled Myrtle Beach Grand Strand. "This will be my crowning glory. I'm going to rename it Franklin Morse Island."

The lawyer shifted his weight uneasily as his eyes darted from Morse to the models and back again. His eyes widened in alarm. *He's as insane as Carl! Why didn't I see it before?*

As if reading his mind, Franklin Morse turned and his intense gaze fell on Harold Wills. "I know what you are thinking. He's crazy. It can't be done. Impossible." He placed his hands on the lawyer's shoulders and leaned in close. "Well, my friend, there is a saying, 'crazy like a fox'. That is exactly what I am. With your help and the unwitting help of all those students whom John Marley recruited, my dream will become reality. And just remember, you will be a very wealthy man when I am through, twenty million dollars wealthy."

Now it was Harold Wills' turn to smile. *If he's crazy, as long as I get my money, he can be crazy anytime he wants.*

80

Before the lawyer could say anything, however, Morse dropped his hands, moved away, and continued, his voice taking on a menacing quality. "Just remember the students in Charleston and Myrtle Beach are not to know anything about their missions until right before they happen." Wills nodded in agreement. "And make sure there are no traces of the students' bodies left on Saturday. I don't want the gentlemen in the other cities to get suspicious."

"I promise you that there will be no slip-ups this time," assured Wills.

Franklin Morse's eyes were hard and as cold as steel on a winter day, his voice barely above a whisper: "There better not be."

Chapter Twenty-Two

Cathy's Home
Two Miles from Wrightsville Beach

An uneasy silence settled in Cathy's living room, each person alone in thought about the sudden disappearance of the students. Finally, Linda broke the silence: "Look, we can't sit around here all day. We'll all go crazy."

David looked over at his fiancée. "Do you have anything specific in mind?" He cocked his head to one side and lifted one eyebrow. "What's going on in that attractive head of yours?"

"Nothing can be done on the case until they find the students. So, why don't we check out the Royal Sea Shell Resort on Shell Island? I want to get another look at the deck overlooking the water since that's where the wedding photos will be shot, and the room next to the restaurant since that's where the reception will be."

"If it doesn't snow," reminded Cathy.

"How often has it snowed here on Christmas?"

Cathy thought for a minute. "Once that I know of. And fourteen inches at that."

"Even if it does, nothing, but nothing is going to ruin that day for me. After all, I am marrying the man of my dreams." The tender look that Linda gave David as she spoke those words would have melted the biggest glacier in the world.

The Surveillance Van

Back in the hidden van, Carl and Omar looked at each other in disgust. "That much mush kind of makes me want to puke," commented Omar.

That crazy gleam once again entered Carl's eyes. "I think I'll ruin their plans, too."

Creases lined Omar's forehead. "Whose plans?"

"Tate and Sokol's"

"What do you mean?" A light suddenly illuminated the ex-con's brain. "Oh, no. You're not thinking of doing what I think you are, are you?"

Carl glared at his companion. "Why not? It will be easy to snatch both women at that gown fitting."

"But why?"

"Because I can."

The alarm in Omar's voice grew. "Mr. Wills isn't going to like this. You know he's not going to approve."

The killer's crazy gleam fixed on Omar. "Then we just won't tell him, will we."

Omar shook his head nervously. "No, of course not."

As soon as Austin left the van, Omar picked up the phone. "Mr. Wills, Carl has decided to......"

Chapter Twenty-Three

Cathy, Linda, David, and Peter dined in the resort restaurant overlooking the Atlantic Ocean and feasted on tuna grilled to perfection, asparagus, baked potatoes, and fresh bread. The group shared a chilled bottle of chardonnay.

The window table afforded them a panoramic view of the water as relentless blue-green waves pounded the shoreline. When Cathy excused herself to use the ladies' room, Peter quickly turned to the others. "If you don't mind, while you two firm up your reception and wedding night plans with the hotel, I'd like to take a walk with Cathy on the beach. There are some things we really need to discuss in private." Looking from face to face, he implored, "I hope you don't mind."

Linda gave David a knowing look. "Not in the least. You go ahead."

Once Peter left the table to wait for Cathy in the lobby, David turned to Linda and asked, "What do you suppose he wants to talk to her about?"

Linda smiled lovingly at her fiancé. "A lot of things my dear, a lot of things." Turning toward the floor-to-ceiling picture windows, she changed subjects. "Won't this be just gorgeous decorated for

Christmas? Can't you see us here one month from now? You will be so handsome in your tux. I can't wait for you to see my dress."

"You still won't tell me what your dress looks like? Won't you at least give me a hint?"

"No way! I want it to be a total surprise." Linda rose and extended her hand to her beloved. "Come on, you. Maybe we can talk the management into letting us see the honeymoon suite."

The Beach Outside the Resort

Cathy and Peter removed their shoes and walked leisurely along the beach. The sun shone brightly, and the sand felt warm between their toes. They passed gray and white seagulls standing at attention in the sand. Overhead, brown pelicans flew in single-file formation. Next to them, the waves rolled in continuous rows to the shore. Beyond the waves, the water sparkled like a giant bright blue topaz.

Cathy sighed contentedly as they hooked pinkie fingers, this time not trying to pull away. Peter, careful to focus on the sea, whispered, "What happened to us, Cathy? I mean I know you were attracted to John Marley, but I always felt some kind of wall between us, even before he entered the picture. It seemed to start as soon as we returned from Disney World. He paused as his brows knitted in concentration. No, that's not quite true. It actually started right after your cat Doc died."

Cathy dropped his hand, stopped abruptly, and turned to face the water. Her face took on a faraway look, and then a great sadness filled her large brown eyes. "It had nothing to do with you or, for that matter, John Marley. Yes, I liked John, but not in the way you think. Oh, I tried to convince you and myself that I did. But if I'm really honest, he was a convenient excuse, a wedge to drive you away."

"But why, Cathy? We had gotten so close in Disney World."

Cathy now turned to face him. "That's just it. We had gotten too close."

Peter put his hand under her chin, forcing her to look up at him, and searched her dark brown eyes with his bright blue ones. "I repeat, why?"

Cathy eased away from Peter. "Disney World is such a magical place that it is easy to get caught up in its fantasies and the world of possibilities."

Peter's face took on a puzzled expression. "I would hardly call the four of us almost being killed fantasy and positive possibility."

Cathy shook her head, her highlighted hair being blown by the wind. "Of course not. I didn't mean that. But the parks themselves allow people of all ages to dream of brighter tomorrows."

Peter now seemed genuinely confused. "What's wrong with that? You've lost me."

Indicating the sand with her hand, Cathy said, "Let's sit down, Peter."

They sat facing each other on the warm, powdery sand. Looking into his eyes, Cathy continued, "You probably won't understand this, but the truth is I live in a world of fear."

Peter searched her eyes. "You mean because of the cancer?" Cathy nodded. "Of course I understand. You forget how we first met."

"I remember, at the cancer support group. But you can't truly understand because you don't live with it. Your wife Peggy understood because she too lived with it, until she died from it."

Peter's voice became adamant, almost defensive. "Don't you think I also lived with the daily fear? Knowing she was dying, I woke up every morning scared to death that I would turn over and find her body cold and stiff."

Gently Cathy stroked his hand. "I know you were scared, but your fear ended with her death. For me and thousands like me, the fear never really ends. Oh, many put up a good front or try to busy themselves so they don't have time to think, but it's always lurking somewhere in the subconscious. Unlike some other cancers, breast cancer survivors are never considered really cured, not even after five years." She paused, and then began again. "Let me try to explain it this way. It's like we're trapped on an island with no way off. There is a force-five hurricane hovering just off shore; it may miss us completely, or it may strike at any time. We can't predict its course, so we've got to be prepared for the worst because—let's face it—a force-five hurricane leaves nothing behind except destruction and death. Remember the destruction of Katrina in New Orleans? Well, that was a force three; think what would have happened if that had come in as a five.

Peter looked at her quizzically. "I understand the metaphor, but I still don't get what this has to do with Disney World or me."

Cathy stood up and began to pace. "Things like Disney World help me forget, if only for a little while, that the hurricane called cancer lurks just off the shore of the island called my life. It's a diversion that stops me from looking offshore. Unfortunately, diversions such as Disney World are only temporary. When they end, and I once again must face the ocean, the dark storm clouds of reality once more crash in. My oncologist put it very plainly. If the cancer comes back, I'm a dead woman!"

Peter stood and brushed the sand from his pants. "What about me? I still don't understand why you tried to push me away after Doc's death?"

Cathy stopped pacing and looked beseechingly into Peter's eyes. "You know that I was devastated by Doc's unexpected death from cancer. My cats are the children I never had. But more than that, they came into my life right after the first mastectomy, when I was at my lowest point. Those dear little gifts from God turned my darkness into light and my tears into laughter. When there was heartache in my first marriage, they gave me unconditional love. And in turn, they allowed me to experience the joy of loving unconditionally. The cats honestly needed me, which gave me a reason to live. Don't you see? Right now, if something happens to me, the only ones I really worry about are the rest of my beloved cats, my family. I worry constantly over what will become of them if I die. If I were to let our relationship go any further, I would worry about you. Doc's death was my wake up call. You've already lost one wife to cancer. I can't, in good conscience, put you in a position where the same thing could happen again, especially after experiencing the excruciating pain of having to watch my beloved little cat waste away from that evil disease. Not to mention the fact that I love you too much to ever want to be a burden to you."

Peter's face and eyes lit up. "Do you realize what you just said?"

Cathy's eyes opened wide and she bit her lip in embarrassment. "I didn't mean to say that."

"It's too late now. You can't take it back." Peter enveloped Cathy in a bear hug. She briefly tried to resist, but he was too strong for her. "I could be diagnosed with cancer tomorrow, be killed in the line of duty, or, for that matter, get hit by a bus. The point is there are no guarantees in life for any of us. Heck, we aren't even guaranteed five minutes from now. All we have is right here and right now. Every minute we have that is free from pain and sorrow is a gift from the Almighty. If we don't reach for the happiness that is ours for the taking this very minute, we waste whatever precious time is left to any of us. I believe the Creator meant for us to live our lives to the fullest, which means taking chances, taking risks. I love you, Cathy Cleveland, and would rather have a day or a week or a month with you than have the rest of my life without you. Yes, I know that when you love this much, if something happens, you also hurt this much. The point is I'm willing to risk it. Are you?" Saying that, he kissed her with a passion so intense that, for a few precious moments, the world around them disappeared.

Cathy's body surrendered to him completely. She raised her face eagerly to his and matched his passion, kiss for kiss. "I love you more than I thought I could love or wanted to love anyone ever again." Peter crushed her to his chest. After a few moments, he started to laugh. Gazing up at him, Cathy asked, "What's so funny?"

He whispered into her hair, "Look around. It seems we have attracted quite a crowd of onlookers."

Hastily, Cathy stepped back. When she looked around and saw at least ten people staring at the two of them, her cheeks burned bright red. She made a feeble attempt to pat her hair down. "We better get back. David and Linda must be wondering what happened to us."

"They know we went for a walk. I told them I wanted to talk to you alone."

Cathy started to walk toward the hotel, but Peter grabbed her hand and pulled her back. "Before we go back, let's get one thing straight."

"What's that?"

"No more trying to push me away, no matter what. Deal?"

Cathy stared deep into his eyes as if trying to see into the future and sighed. Suddenly the tension between them was as thick as a heavy blanket of fog. Slowly, she extended her hand. "Deal!"

The tension dissolved into laughter. The pair shook hands and walked arm-in-arm back to the hotel. Linda and David met them at the outdoor pool. "You should see the honeymoon suite. It has the most unbelievable view of the beach and the ocean," bubbled Linda.

Jabbing Linda in the side, David broke in. "You two look like cats that just ate a whole can of tuna."

Linda stepped back, tilted her head, and scrutinized her friends. "David's right. What's going on?"

Peter winked at Cathy. "We finally cleared up a little misunderstanding."

"We sure did!" Cathy agreed, winking back.

"Hey, what's going on?" a bewildered David asked, looking from Peter to Cathy.

Catching the wink, Linda tugged at her lover's arm. "Never mind, sweetheart. I'll explain it to you later."

Chapter Twenty-Four

Warehouse
Near Wilmington International Airport
Wednesday Night

Harold Wills sat behind a desk in one of the warehouse offices and chewed on his fingernails. Things were not going as planned. Gazing at the young men, he couldn't shake this uneasy feeling. *They're becoming restless. How am I supposed to keep them in line for three more days?* He focused on two young men in particular. Wills couldn't quite remember their names, but they had given him a bad feeling from the very first day. He thought about his accomplices: *Carl has gotten totally unmanageable.* He thought about Franklin Morse: *That man is ruthless.* He thought about the money: *Nice, but I can't spend it in jail or dead. Is all this really worth it? I'm just not sure anymore. I need to think!*

Chapter Twenty-Five

Cathy's Home
Two Miles from Wrightsville Beach
Thursday Morning, Thanksgiving Day

Cathy awoke with a smile on her face. Peter had slept on Cathy's couch Wednesday night. She wasn't being prudish but wanted their first time together to be when they were alone in the house. She also felt nervous about what his initial reaction would be to seeing her chest. Having had complications with the first mastectomy, one side of her chest was badly scarred. It looked like a dry riverbed with several tributaries branching off the main one. She had explained all this to Peter last night after Linda had suggested he stay since they were going to spend Thanksgiving together. The man had been so sweet and understanding and had said just the right thing, assuring her that he would never push her into anything, waiting instead until she was ready. He told her that he had fallen for the beauty that was within and that the outside didn't matter.

Last evening the foursome had gone to church to thank God for all the blessings they had to be grateful for. Peter Channing had definitely topped her list. After church the two couples had returned to Cathy's house and spent the rest of the evening listening to soft music and watching the flames dance in the fireplace. It had been a relaxing time, free of any serious talk.

This morning she repeated her list of blessings. The man again topped the list, followed closely by health, cats, family, and friends.

Cathy moved her feet under the covers and three cats immediately pounced. She propped herself up on one hand, using her other hand to scratch Sneezy behind the ears. He rewarded her with a loud purr. "Even you guys have calmed down and finally come out from under the bed." She yawned and stretched. "Well, I better get up if we want to eat at a reasonable hour." Cathy tiptoed through the living room trailed by six cats demanding their breakfast. "Shsh," she commanded as a loud chorus of meows filled the kitchen. "We don't want to wake Peter."

By the time her guests awoke, the felines were fed and the turkey was in the oven. "Why don't we walk down to the donut shop for breakfast?" suggested David.

The others quickly agreed and set off down the road. Passing the vacant house, Peter noticed the van parked in the back. "How long has that van been parked there? I never noticed it before."

"I have no idea. That house has been empty for a long time."

"Maybe we should check it out," commented David.

The two men turned and started to approach the van. Linda reached out and tugged at David's arm. "Would you two stop playing detectives all the time? This is a holiday, remember? Let's just have a normal day for once. Please?"

Both sheepishly agreed. "Okay. But tomorrow we check it out." The men looked at each other in astonishment after finishing the statements in unison, then turned back toward the road and continued toward the donut shop. Even their actions were in perfect synchronization.

The women's mouths dropped open. "You two are starting to think more and more alike," marveled Linda. "It's almost scary."

Inside the Surveillance Van

Omar watched with bated breath and gun in hand as the two men approached the van, breathing a sigh of relief only when the group was back on the road. *Oh oh, that was too close. They were paying entirely too much attention to this van.* He nervously dialed the number to the warehouse. "Carl? Good, I'm glad you answered the phone."

Carl could hear the urgency in Omar's voice. "What's the matter?"

"It's Sokol and Channing. They started to take an interest in this van."

"What do you mean interest?"

"I mean they looked like they were going to check us out."

"But they didn't?"

"No, but I think they still might."

"Move the van before they come back."

"Where do you want me to move it to?"

Carl thought for a moment. "There are woods behind Cleveland's house. Try to drive it into there. If you can't, just find a place to keep it out of sight, but still within listening distance. Call me when you've moved it."

Omar hung up and drove around to the woods. Finding a clearing large enough to slip the van through, he drove until the vehicle was far enough back from the house that it would not be easily spotted. "Okay, Channing, see if you can find me now," the ex-con chuckled. Picking up the phone, he once again dialed Carl.

Cathy's House

Walking back, the four once again passed the vacant house. "Oh, look, the van's gone," commented Linda. "Maybe they were just some kids making out or doing something slightly illegal."

"It's as if they knew what we were thinking," mused David.

"Whatever they were doing, they're gone now." Cathy turned away from the vacant house. "I hope you know that this Thanksgiving dinner is going to be a group effort."

Linda put her arm through Cathy's. "We wouldn't have it any other way. Would we, boys?" Her tone left no room for argument.

"No ma'am!!" Again both men were in perfect synchronization.

Chapter Twenty-Six

The Surveillance Van
The Woods behind Cathy's House
Thursday Afternoon

Carl burst through the door of the van with a plate full of turkey, stuffing, mashed potatoes, cranberries, and green bean casserole. "I even brought you pumpkin pie for dessert."

"Thanks," said a grateful Omar, reaching hungrily for the plate.

"You should see the spread at the warehouse! This is only part of what Mr. Wills brought in for the boys. He's making sure they're very happy today." Cutthroat Carl snickered. "They don't know it, but they're condemned men and this is like their last meal, only they still have two days to live." He looked around. "Can you still hear them from here?"

"Good enough."

"Anything new to report?"

"Not really. The four sat down to dinner a little while ago." Suddenly, through the receiver, they could hear Cathy's phone ringing.

"Put the phone tap on loud speaker."

Omar did as he was told. The voice on the other end of the line was that of Emma Grayson.

Inside Cathy's House

"Cathy, I'm sorry to bother you at home on a holiday, but I thought you would want to know the result of the autopsy on your friend. The coroner has ruled his death an accident. John Marley's remains are to be flown to Iowa in the morning." Back in the van, Carl and Omar grinned at each other.

Cathy was incredulous. "After everything else that has happened, you don't really believe that do you?"

"No, of course not." Unfortunately, with his death ruled accidental, we can't actively investigate his killing, but we can still investigate the suspected breach of homeland security."

The college instructor thanked her for calling, wished her a "Happy Thanksgiving," and hung up. She filled the others in on the conversation.

Turning to Peter, Linda asked, "What do you make of that?"

"I would have been surprised had his death been ruled anything other than an accident. Carl Austin is a professional, not an amateur. I read the file on him. He makes very few mistakes." The agent walked over to Cathy and placed his hand on her shoulder. "We'll get him, Cathy. I promise you that." Turning to David he said, "Come on, let's see who's winning the football game."

The Van in the Woods

Carl grinned from ear to ear. "Thank you very much, Peter Channing, for the compliment. Tomorrow, you will experience first hand just how good I really am."

Franklin Morse's Study

Harold Wills was ushered into Franklin Morse's study. The industrialist entered wearing a tuxedo. "This had better be important. As you can see, I have a house full of dinner guests."

95

"It is, I assure you," beamed the lawyer.

"Well then, what is it?"

"The autopsy came in. The coroner declared Marley's death an accident."

"For this you interrupted my party?"

A slightly flustered Harold Wills replied, "I thought you would be pleased?"

A butler appeared at the door with two flutes of champagne, but before the attorney could reach out for one, Morse waved the servant away. "I shall be pleased when and only when Saturday goes off flawlessly." The industrialist started for the door. "Now I need to return to my guests, and I suggest you return to the warehouse and keep your young guests happy." At the doorway he stopped and turned toward Wills. "For security reasons, I would suggest that you not visit me here again until after Saturday. Is that clear?"

"Perfectly, sir."

"You can show yourself out." Morse left Wills alone in the study.

That bastard! I am the only one who knows his identity. If something goes wrong, there is no way to link this to him, only to me. Carl and Omar only know me. The boys have only seen me. Even the warehouse is leased to a dummy corporation through me. What I need is a little insurance, a little bargaining power if things go wrong.

Quietly Harold Wills slipped out of the study, but instead of walking to the front door, crossed to the room where Morse had taken him earlier. As he tried the handle, a butler again appeared at his elbow. He jumped back slightly. "Champagne, sir?"

Wills accepted the champagne flute. "Thank you." Sipping champagne and keeping a wary eye on the butler, the lawyer pretended to study the priceless art works that adorned the walls of the hallway. As soon as the butler left, he again tried the door. It was locked. "We'll see about this." Wills put the still half-full flute on a side table, walked out the front door, and down the steps to his car. Opening the glove compartment, he removed the digital camera that was always kept there. Smiling to himself, he murmured, "Just for such emergencies."

Stealthily, Wills slipped around to the back of the house. Because of the party going on, the guard dogs had been locked up. While the front of the house looked like a southern mansion, the back was built for optimum views of the water. The entire back of the house was glass, with a deck off the second floor and a terrace off the first. He found the floor-to-ceiling windows of the room with the large table. Using the zoom lens, Wills focused on the models and began snapping away. Suddenly a voice behind him demanded, "What are you doing?"

Wills turned, half expecting to see Marcus. Instead, it was an unfamiliar security guard. Taking a gamble, the attorney responded, "This is my first time here at a party. I'm so impressed by its grandeur that I wanted to take some pictures. I hope that's all right." The counterfeit party guest handed the camera to the security guard. "If not, I'll be happy to give you the memory card."

Uncertain now, the guard tried to look in the window, but without the benefit of the zoom on the camera and with the glare on the glass from the sunlight, could only see the table and vague shapes in silhouette. The guard did not want to insult a guest of his employer so instead of confiscating the camera he simply handed it back and said, "You can keep what you've taken but take no more until I check with the head of security."

"Of course," bluffed Wills. "Thank you."

By the time the guard returned with the head of security, Wills was long gone. "He must have returned to the party," stammered the new guard.

"You idiot!" growled Marcus. "Let's go." The two searched the large house but found no sign of the man with the camera.

They walked back outside and stopped on the front porch. "Describe him," demanded the security chief. When he had, Marcus knew exactly who the photographer had been. "Show me which window!" The nervous guard did as he was told. Marcus grimaced. "Stay here and let no one else near this window."

The head of security entered the main dining room and quietly sidled up to Franklin Morse. "We may have a problem." Describing what had just transpired, he asked his boss for instructions.

"Get that camera!"

Chapter Twenty-Seven

Today, after a quick breakfast of cold cereal, orange-mango juice and coffee, the men and the women were going their separate ways. This morning the women needed to pick out flowers and sample wedding cake. In the afternoon they were scheduled to have their final gown fittings. The men's first stop would be the travel agency to finalize the honeymoon plans, and then in the afternoon they were having their tuxes fitted. The four decided to meet at TideWater for lunch. TideWater was a delightful restaurant that sat on the bank of the Intracoastal Waterway.

Peter hugged Cathy just as she was about to open the car door. "I'm still not too keen on you going anywhere without me until this business is settled."

Cathy hugged Peter in return, but pulled away just enough to look into his eyes. "I thought we settled this at breakfast. I am not going to be alone today. Linda will watch me like a hawk. Remember?"

Peter reluctantly released her. "All right. But stay together no matter what!"

C.C. grinned impishly. "Yes, Daddy." Before Peter could think of a snappy reply, Cathy jumped in the car and shut the door.

The women set off for The Rose Garden, a floral shop that specialized in rose floral arrangements Since the wedding itself was going to be in front of the fireplace in Cathy's living room at midnight on Christmas Eve, the two chose six dozen long stem red and white roses to be placed in vases around the living room. The flowers would then be moved to the resort for the Christmas afternoon reception.

The plan for the wedding was to attend the eleven p.m. Christmas Eve service at the tiny church at the end of Cathy's street. After church the minister had agreed to come to Cathy's home to perform the simple private ceremony. Only the four of them plus the minister would be in attendance. The fireplace, the Christmas tree adorned with old-fashioned bubble lights, twinkle lights around the minibar, and scented candles scattered on tables throughout the room would light the living room. The newlyweds would spend the rest of their wedding night at the resort where a reception attended by David's and Linda's families, coworkers, and other acquaintances would follow on Christmas afternoon. Several of their friends without children or whose children were grown had already booked rooms at the hotel for the entire holiday.

After the flower shop, the women's next stop was the resort. They selected the reception dinner menu consisting of an appetizer of fresh shrimp on ice, followed by an entrée of roast turkey, honey baked ham, sweet potatoes, mashed potatoes, green bean casserole, spinach salad, and rolls. Champagne would flow out of a fountain to be set in the middle of the room. For those who chose not to drink, sparkling grape juice would be available, as well as coffee and tea.

Linda and Cathy's final stop was at Carla's Cakes & Cookies Bakeshop. The women both agreed that this bakery's cakes were the best they had ever tasted. Linda chose a four-tier white cake with chocolate pudding filling. The icing would be their delicious butter cream frosting with red roses cascading down each layer. For the top, instead of the standard bride and groom, she chose a pair of swans gliding on a mirrored pond. "That is going to be just gorgeous," sighed a slightly envious Cathy.

* * *

David and Peter set off for the travel agency. At first David and Linda had thought about going back to Florida for their honeymoon but decided to postpone that trip in the hope that they could convince Peter and Cathy to go back with them the following summer.

David had insisted on picking the new honeymoon destination himself so he could surprise Linda. All he would tell her is that she needed to pack for warm weather. It turned out that he had actually picked two locations. The day after Christmas, the two of them would fly to Las Vegas for a three-day stay. From there, they would fly on to the island of Kauai, one of the Hawaiian Islands, for a week of snorkeling, hiking, and sightseeing.

After the men exited the travel agency, Peter slapped David on the back. "I congratulate you on your choice for a honeymoon. Linda is going to be ecstatic."

Peter checked his watch before opening the car door. He glanced at David over the roof of the car, and then slid into the passenger seat. "Look, we've still got an hour before we're supposed to meet the girls. Do you mind if we make one more stop?"

"No problem. Where to?" asked David as he backed the car out of the parking space.

"I'd like to head over to the mall."

David glanced over at his friend. "We're going there this afternoon for the tux fitting."

"I know, but I'd really like to do this now."

"Do what now?" David glanced in both directions, then eased the car forward.

Peter took a deep breath. "I want to look for an engagement ring!"

"What?" exclaimed David, stomping on the brake, which, in turn, threw both men forward. He put the car in park and turned to give his full attention to his friend. "Have you asked her?"

"Not yet; I plan to tonight. I want to have the ring with me when I do. I figure if I find one this morning, then maybe they can have it sized by this afternoon."

"How do you know Cathy's ring size?"

Peter reached in his pocket and pulled out a sapphire ring. "I sneaked into her jewelry box this morning and borrowed this. She wears it occasionally on her left hand so I know it fits."

Once more shifting the car into gear and stepping on the gas, David chuckled. "Clever boy. But, if you don't mind, I know a jeweler here in Wilmington that has rings like no others. In fact, it was Cathy who first took me there when I was looking for an engagement ring for Linda."

"What's the name of it?"

"Tavernay's, over on Wrightsville Avenue."

"I've heard the name before at work. And from what I hear, you're right about the jewelry. Let's go there instead."

"You've got it."

The Warehouse

Carl paced the warehouse like a caged panther. He kept rubbing his hands together with anticipation, the maniacal gleam back in his eyes. He couldn't wait for this afternoon. The young men sitting around the room stared at him uneasily. They knew something was up, but what, they had no idea.

Harold Wills kept a wary eye on Carl. He had tried to dissuade him from grabbing Linda Tate as well as Cathy Cleveland, but Cutthroat Carl was beyond the point of reasoning so he had backed off. Harold knew enough about Carl Austin to know when it was time to give him some leeway. The lawyer stole another glance at his associate. *He does get the jobs done that he is paid for. And this will, after all, be his last job for me, or anyone else for that matter.* Wills smiled to himself. He was beginning to feel better about things. *After this job, Carl will be gone. If things go well, I will be wealthy beyond my wildest dreams. If not, I have those pictures, now secure in a safety deposit box with instructions to my lawyer to turn them over to the Feds if anything happens to me.*

The Study of Franklin Morse

Marcus entered Franklin Morse's study. The big man stood in front of the floor-to-ceiling windows looking out at the water beyond, his hands clasped behind his back. "You sent for me, sir?"

"What's the status of the camera?" asked the billionaire without turning around.

"Getting the camera was no problem. I found it in his glove compartment."

"Good." Morse turned to face his subordinate. "Did you destroy it?"

Marcus shook his head no.

The sound from Franklin Morse's mouth sounded more like a roll of thunder than a human voice. "Why not?"

"Unfortunately, Wills already had prints made before I could get to it. He stashed them in a safety deposit box somewhere. I have been making discreet inquiries. I'll find them. In the meantime, I thought it wiser not to take the camera and tip him off that we are on to him." Marcus confidently added, "I did, however, replace the memory card with one of my own."

Ignoring Marcus's last remark, Morse crossed to his chair and sat down heavily. He grabbed a pencil from its leather container and tapped impatiently on the mahogany desk. "We're running out of time." He leaned back in his chair, twirling the pencil between his fingers. "I've got another job for you. Tomorrow night, once Carl, the students, and the women are all disposed of, I want you to eliminate Omar, and Wills too. Wills' death must look like an accident. Whatever you do, make sure it looks like Harold Wills was the mastermind behind all this. That way there is no trail that will even remotely lead to me."

"What if things go wrong tomorrow?" asked Marcus.

Franklin Morse's face turned to stone. "Then eliminate them all immediately."

"What about your other projects in Charleston and Myrtle Beach?"

The tycoon shrugged. "I'll find others to lead those."

Marcus raised an eyebrow. "With the same ending for them?"

Morse smiled a lazy sort of smile and continued to play with the pencil in his hands. "Of course. That way no one lives long enough to tell anything."

The chief of security nodded and forced a smile. *And what about me?*

David's Car

David and Peter left Tavernay's Jewelers like giddy schoolboys. In Peter's left pocket was a black velvet ring box containing an exquisite one-carat round-cut diamond engagement ring set in a combination of white and yellow gold. The diamond solitaire had a matching wedding band that encircled the large diamond with smaller ones.

Peter had lucked out. The moment he saw it, the love-smitten agent knew it was made for his lady. It was even the right size. He couldn't wait to give it to her. *Not at lunch, though,* he thought. *I'll give it to her tonight when we are alone. Maybe I'll take her back to the beach for a walk, or maybe in front of her fireplace after David and Linda go to bed.*

So engrossed was he in his daydream that he didn't hear David asking, "So when are you going to pop the question?"

The agent looked dazedly over at David. "I'm sorry. What did you say?"

David shook his head. "I want to know when you are going to ask her."

"Tonight sometime, when we're alone." Focused now, Peter continued, "Promise me you won't say a word to Linda."

"I promise."

"Swear to it!"

"I swear. Believe me, I know that if Linda were to find out, Cathy would know something was up immediately and would badger her unmercifully until she told. This is just between you and Cathy until she says yes."

"You don't think I jumped the gun in buying this, do you?" Peter asked, a hint of doubt entering his voice.

"Of course not. I know she loves you. She'll say yes. I'm sure of it."

Peter again took the ring out of its box and slowly turned it between his fingers. The man watched as it sparkled, tiny ribbons of color shooting out as the sun caught each of its many facets. "I hope she likes the ring."

David looked over in mock exasperation. "Would you stop? You are Peter Channing, cool, confident FBI agent, not Peter Channing, insecure, lovesick school boy."

Peter laughed sheepishly and placed the ring back in its box and the box back in his pocket.

Chapter Twenty-Eight

TideWater Restaurant
Next to the Intracoastal Waterway
Friday Afternoon

Lunch at the TideWater was a jovial affair. Everyone was in a great mood. The restaurant had a choice of seating, either on the sun deck or in a second floor glassed-in sunroom. Because a stiff breeze was blowing off the water, the four opted for the second floor. Through the large picture windows, Cathy, David, and Linda watched as majestic cabin cruisers and magnificent sail boats slowly made their way up and down the Intracoastal Waterway. Peter, however, couldn't take his eyes off Cathy. Finally, she turned to him and asked, "What is it?"

"What is what?" asked Peter feigning innocence.

"You keep staring at me. Why? Is there something on my face?"

Peter laughed. "There is nothing on your face. I just happen to find you very attractive so I love looking at you."

Cathy rolled her twinkling eyes in mock irritation. "Well, quit it. You're making me self conscious."

David watched the exchange between Cathy and Peter with a barely suppressed grin on his face. When Peter glanced at him, David winked. Linda caught the wink and laid her fork down with a bang. "Okay, I saw that!"

"Saw what?" asked David innocently.

"Saw that wink, that's what! I want to know exactly what is going on!!!"

"Patience, sweetheart," answered the airline pilot sweetly. "You'll know soon enough."

Cathy turned her head and looked at both men shrewdly. "Then there is something going on?"

Peter patted her hand. "Later, darling."

Cathy's eyebrows shot up. "Darling? Since when do you call me darling?"

"Since just now." He leaned into her, gazing deeply into her eyes. "It's a surprise. I promise you will know tonight. All right?"

Cathy looked over at Linda and crossed her eyes, then turned back at Peter and pretended to pout, "All right."

The Parking Lot of Dreams of Elegance Bridal Salon

After making sure the young men had eaten lunch and had a new set of movies to watch, Carl left for Dreams of Elegance Bridal Salon. He wanted to be in position long before the women arrived. Parking his SUV in the lot behind the boutique, Carl settled down to wait, licking his lips in anticipation. "It won't be long now," he murmured.

Chapter Twenty-Nine

TideWater Restaurant
Next to the Intracoastal Waterway

Before the two couples went their separate ways, they agreed to meet at the Oceanside, a beautiful restaurant located on the ocean at Wrightsville Beach, for dinner at six o'clock. . Normally Cathy liked to dine there on Sunday mornings after church. The restaurant had a wonderful Sunday brunch. When the weather permitted, she enjoyed eating on the pier, watching the surfers, swimmers, and sun worshipers. Earlier in the fall, Cathy had introduced Peter to that pleasure. It had quickly become one of their favorite weekly traditions.

Tonight, however, Peter had a plan. After dinner, he and his beloved would take a stroll along the beach. There, in the moonlight, under the starlit sky, he would ask Cathy to spend the rest of her life with him. He could hardly wait.

The men had a two o'clock appointment at the tux shop in the mall. It was already almost 1:30, so they said their hasty good-byes at the restaurant and left. The women decided to stay and linger over another cup of coffee since their appointment wasn't until 2:30. "The guys were acting so strange at lunch. What do you suppose that was all about?" asked Cathy.

Linda's eyes sparkled. "I'm not positive, but I think I know."

Cathy looked at her friend quizzically, "What?"

The computer analyst shook her head. "If you can't figure it out, then I'm not going to say." She paused and tugged on the brown and beige scarf draped around her neck in contemplation. "Besides, I could be wrong. We'll just wait until tonight."

The Mall

Peter and David lifted their arms as the tailor measured first one and then the other. The men would be wearing black tuxes with white shirts, red cummerbunds, and red bow ties. Small red roses would accent their lapels. "You know, if I had my way, we'd just wait and get married at one of those quickie wedding chapels in Las Vegas," grumbled David.

His best man laughed. "Just keep telling yourself that you are doing this for Linda. After all, this is going to be her first and only trip down the aisle."

"But that's just it, there isn't even going to be an aisle."

Peter jabbed his friend in the ribs. "You know what I mean."

The groom grinned at their reflections in the mirror. "I know. What kind of a wedding do you suppose Cathy will want?"

Peter thought for a moment. "Probably something small and private since this is her second time around. Who knows, maybe we'll do the Vegas wedding chapel thing."

"Lucky you! Ouch!!" David jumped as the tailor accidentally poked him with a pin.

Dreams of Elegance Bridal Salon

The women walked into the busy bridal salon precisely at 2:30. "Hello, Ms. Cleveland. Hello, Ms. Tate," gushed the shop owner as she rushed to welcome Linda. "I have both your gowns waiting for you ladies. Ms. Tate, your gown is in dressing room three, Ms. Cleveland in room four. Unfortunately, as you can see, we are quite busy today. It will be a few moments before a seamstress can work with you."

"That's no problem," the bride assured the sales woman. "We have all afternoon."

The women walked to the back of the salon and down the hallway that led to the dressing rooms. At the end of the hallway was the delivery entrance to the shop. "That's odd," commented Cathy.

"What's odd?"

Cathy eyed the door suspiciously. "We've been here what, maybe four or five times?"

"Umm, four—once to pick out the fabric, another to approve the patterns they made, a third to okay the working models, and last Saturday to fit the actual gowns. That makes this our fifth visit."

Cathy gestured toward the end of the hallway. "I've never seen that door open before."

Her friend shrugged. "Maybe they had a delivery and the delivery person didn't shut it." Reaching dressing room three, Linda turned to Cathy, "Would you come in and help me get the gown over my head?"

The matron of honor curtseyed. "That's what a matron-of-honor or maid-of-honor is for. You know, I still can't figure out what I am."

Linda giggled then opened the door to the dressing room. There stood Carl with a revolver in his hand. The giggle in Linda's throat died and both women instinctively stepped back. "Don't move, ladies, and don't scream."

Linda immediately recognized Carl Austin from his picture. "What do you want?"

Carl laughed his mirthless laugh. "That should be obvious. You two, of course." Indicating the open door with his revolver he barked, "Let's go."

Desperately Cathy and Linda looked around for someone to notice as they slowly walked to the service entrance. No one did. Linda tried a diversionary tactic. "Gee, from your dossier, I thought you only used knives to kill people with."

"Oh, I use guns on occasion too. Keep moving, Miss Tate." The killer prodded Linda in the back with his gun.

The women exited the building. Cathy pretended to stumble and dropped her purse next to the loading dock. Angrily, Carl gripped her elbow and roughly shoved her forward. They were hustled into Carl's SUV. There he first made Linda tie Cathy's hands and feet with duct tape, and then he tied Linda's. "This is just so you don't get some silly notion of trying to get the jump on me while I'm driving. And don't think you can jump out of the car at a light. This car is equipped with those child protection locks that are controlled from the front seat." He chuckled, "They were such a great invention for people in my line of work."

As Carl pulled out of the driveway, Cathy and Linda saw a woman getting out of her car. Because their hands were tied behind their backs they couldn't pound on the window, but they screamed as loud as they could, bouncing up and down as they did so. Carl immediately turned the car radio up full blast. The woman glanced over and, since her view was obscured by the tinted windows, assumed that the screams came from the radio. Glaring, she shook her head in disgust.

Carl looked amused as he adjusted his rear view mirror. "Nice try, ladies."

Chapter Thirty

The Warehouse
Near Wilmington International Airport

Six pairs of resentful eyes stared at the trio when the killer entered the warehouse with the women. One pair of eyes filled with anguish, the eyes of the young man named Timothy. Earlier in the week he was the one who had expressed doubt about killing the innocent people on the island.

Harold Wills hurried out of one of the warehouse offices and motioned Carl to bring the women into it. "You idiot!! Why did you parade the women in front of those guys? You should have brought them in the side entrance."

"What's the difference?" growled a scowling Carl.

"Because now you have given the boys specific faces to attach to what they are about to do."

"So?"

Wills sighed and continued as if lecturing a child: "It is always much easier to kill when the victims are faceless. It gives killing a feeling of unreality. Once you look into someone's eyes, killing becomes more difficult."

"Not for me."

Wills' patience was wearing thin. "Well lucky for the rest of the world, there are not many men like you who take so much pleasure in killing just for killing's sake."

"And where would pansies like you and your boss be without real men like me to do your dirty work? Before Harold Wills could respond, the killer glanced toward the women. "What do you want me to do with them?"

"Untie their hands and put them in the office next door." Turning to Linda and Cathy he continued, "There are two couches in there that you can sleep on and there is a private bathroom in there as well. There are, however, no windows so escape is impossible. You'll get dinner in about an hour. I've already put a few books and magazines in there that I thought might interest you."

"The only thing that would interest us is to know what is going on," Linda spat.

"And why you killed John Marley and are holding all these students," added Cathy.

"I didn't kill John Marley."

Struggling with her bonds, Linda stared incredulously into the eyes of the lawyer. "It's a matter of semantics."

Glancing over her shoulder at Carl Austin, then back at Wills, Cathy pressed the issue. "Okay, maybe you didn't actually drive the nails into his body, but I'm sure you arranged it. I repeat my question. Why? Why all of this?"

"Sorry, ladies. Those questions I can't answer. But I can assure you these gentlemen are here of their own free will." The lawyer motioned to Carl.

Austin did as he was told and then returned. "Why were you so nice to the women when they're just going to die tomorrow anyway?"

The lawyer rolled his eyes before answering. "People who know they are going to die become desperate and will attempt anything. After all, they know they have nothing to lose. But, if you let them believe they are not going to be killed, they are more apt to do what you say and not try anything heroic."

Cutthroat Carl took his knife out and his eyes glittered. "I'd rather watch the fear in people's eyes when they know they only have a few hours to live."

The head man shook his head in frustration. "Put that thing away and do as you're told."

The killer slowly turned the knife toward Wills' chest and stared into the man's eyes, howling with laughter as the color drained from his boss's face. The laughter subsided slowly and he returned the knife to its sheath. "Do you honestly think I would use this thing on you before I've been paid?" His voice took on a barely hidden angry edge. "Especially since I still don't know who is really pulling the strings."

Anger replaced fear and the attorney's voice quivered with rage as he grabbed Carl by his shirt collar and pulled him to within an inch of his face. "And you never will so don't you ever do that again." With his last words he shoved Carl away.

The crazy villain's eyes glistened but he said nothing. *No one touches me. When this is over you will die, just like the rest. It will be a pleasure to watch you beg for mercy.*

Cathy and Linda closely examined the office they were locked in. "This is a déjà vu nightmare. It's just like the office we were locked in at Disney World," complained Cathy as she finally flopped onto one of the couches.

"Only worse," stated Linda flatly as she exited the bathroom.

Cathy looked up at her friend. "How could it be any worse?"

"There are no scissors here to use as a weapon, nothing even remotely sharp. The only things in the bathroom are two toothbrushes and a tube of toothpaste."

Cathy raised an eyebrow. "Two? It's like they were expecting us."

Linda slowly settled in beside her friend on the couch. "Of course they were. Didn't you hear what that guy said about the magazines? But how did they know we would be at the bridal shop today and how did they even know when?" She began to think out loud. "I suppose they could have called the shop and gotten our schedule."

Cathy shook her head. "I don't think the bridal shop would give out that kind of information. No, it's more like they've been listening in on our conversations."

"But how?" Linda repeated.

Both women stared at the floor then suddenly turned toward each other. "The cats," Cathy almost shouted.

"Of course!! They bugged your house. That's why your cats were hiding the night John Marley was killed. These bastards have been listening in to all our conversations." The computer analyst leaned back and closed her eyes. "We can only pray David and Peter will figure it out before they give away anything else at the house."

"But what is this all about? "We still don't have a clue as to what these people are up to."

"We know it's nothing good, that's for sure."

Timothy marched up to Mr. Wills. "What are those women doing here? And why were they tied up like that?"

Placing a hand on the young man's shoulder and trying to use his best fatherly tone, the attorney answered, "Nothing for you to be concerned about."

Shrugging off Wills' hand, Timothy persisted. "Look, I can tell from their dress that they are not part of the rich elite. Why did you have their hands tied?"

"They were just in the wrong place at the wrong time." Wills' tone was almost patronizing.

Gazing toward the locked door, Tim asked, "What are you going to do with them?"

"We'll just try to reason with them and make them see our side; then after tomorrow night we'll let them go."

"What if they don't see our side?"

"Well, then we'll just have to do what we have to do, now won't we."

Tim started to argue then abruptly changed his mind. He noticed Carl listening in on the conversation and saw the suspicious look in his eyes. "Yeah, sure," the young man mumbled instead.

Mr. Wills put his arm around Tim again and walked him back to the area with the pool table. "Don't worry about those women, son. They'll be just fine."

Tim stared at the floor and said nothing. *This is all wrong. I've got to get out of here.*

After Wills left Tim with the other young men, he walked back to his office. Passing Carl, he leaned over and whispered, "Keep an eye on that kid."

Stroking his knife in its sheath, Cutthroat Carl's eyes gleamed. "I already am."

Chapter Thirty-One

Peter and David sat patiently in the Oceanside bar, waiting for Cathy and Linda. Sipping on a margarita, Peter kept one eye on the door. For the tenth time since he had arrived, Peter felt in his pocket for the ring case. David chuckled. "If you don't stop feeling that thing, by the time you give it to Cathy the velvet will be worn off of it."

Peter grinned sheepishly. "You're right." Checking his watch, he frowned slightly. "They are now a half an hour late."

David shrugged. "Maybe the Wrightsville Beach Bridge is up. Let's give them a few more minutes."

Another fifteen minutes went by. David looked over at his friend. "Maybe they got held up with the fittings. Why don't I call the shop and check?" He asked the bartender for a phone book and looked up the number. Slipping his cell phone out of his pocket, the airline pilot dialed the number and listened. A scowl formed on his face. He hit the end button on the phone. "The shop closed over an hour ago. I'll try Linda's cell." David pushed the rapid dial number for Linda's cell phone and listened. Shaking his head, he said, "I'm just getting her voicemail."

Peter took out his cell phone. "Wouldn't you know, my battery is dead."

David glanced over at Peter. "Give me Cathy's cell number and I'll try her phone." He hit end and dialed Cathy's number. "No luck."

Peter's face brightened. "Try her home phone. I'll bet they're there. I almost forgot that Cathy has to feed her cats. Knowing her, she wouldn't want to make them wait for dinner just because she was out having a good time."

David laughed, "She doesn't mind making us wait, but never the cats." He dialed the number, but got the answer machine. His smile vanished. "Uh uh."

Peter got up and reached for his wallet to pay for their drinks. "Since you're staying there, did Cathy give you a key to her house, by any chance?"

The pilot took out his key ring. "Yeah, I've got it right here. Why?"

"Let's go back to the house. Maybe we can at least tell if the women have been there." Placing the money on the bar the FBI agent said to his friend, "I still don't know why neither one of them has called us."

"Maybe the batteries on their cell phones are also dead."

"Both of them?"

Cathy's House

The dark house and empty cat food bowls said it all. "Linda and Cathy obviously haven't been here," said Peter as he turned on a kitchen light. Hearing familiar voices, one by one the cats came out of hiding and rubbed against the men's ankles. Reaching down to scratch Dopey's ear, Peter asked, "What's the matter, didn't your mistress come home and feed you tonight?" He walked into the laundry room and retrieved two cans of soft cat food and two cups of dry. "Don't worry, guys, I'll feed you." Mixing the food together, he spooned a serving into each of the six bowls.

David sat at the counter and watched Peter. Placing his chin in his hands and biting his lower lip, he asked, "Now what? Any ideas?"

Peter sighed philosophically. "Maybe they got hung up with more wedding details."

"Why don't they answer their cell phones? I can believe that maybe one of their phones is dead, but not both." David was starting to worry about his beloved fiancée.

"The batteries could be dead."

David eyed Cathy's answer machine. "The light's flashing. Cathy has a few messages."

Peter glanced at the machine. "It says she has three. Well we know one of the three messages is from us."

David visibly brightened. "Do you think maybe one of the other two messages could be from the girls to us?"

"There's only one way to find out." Peter pressed the play button. "I don't think she'll mind if we listen to her messages."

The last message was indeed from the guys, but the first two messages sent chills up the men's spines. Both were from the bridal shop. The first call was from the shop owner apologizing for the women's obvious inconvenience at having to wait, which resulted in their leaving before being fitted. She then asked when they wished to reschedule their fittings. The second call from the shop was even more alarming. This time it was to let Cathy know that her purse had been found outside the back door to the shop. "Your money and credit cards are still in the wallet so I don't think anything was stolen. I'll leave your purse at the front counter and you can pick it up at your convenience." The message ended and the machine beeped.

The men stared at each other in horror. Peter quickly picked up the phone and dialed headquarters. Identifying himself, he asked for Ms. Emma Grayson. The agent knew his superior often worked late into the evening and only hoped that tonight would be one of those nights. The supervisor answered on the third ring. Peter skipped the usual pleasantries and got right to the point. When he finished, she asked quietly, "Which shop?" Not knowing anything about the shop, Peter handed the phone to David who gave Ms. Grayson the name and location of the bridal salon. After jotting down the information, she ordered the men to stay at the house. "A team of agents will be over shortly. Once the premises are thoroughly searched, we'll make Ms. Cleveland's house the base of operations until the women are found."

The men hung up the phone and just stared at each other. Finally Peter broke the silence. "It's like they've known from the start what our every move was going to be. But how?"

The Van

Omar danced around inside the van now hidden safely in the woods. The FBI was going to set up a temporary headquarters in the house. That meant he would hear every plan they made. *Mr. Wills is going to like this. Yes indeed, he's definitely going to like this.*

Chapter Thirty-Two

Cathy's House
Two Miles from Wrightsville Beach

David paced the room like a caged tiger. As the pacing began to wear on Peter's nerves, he pretended a calm he didn't feel and quietly said, "There is nothing we can do until the team arrives, so why don't you just have a seat."

David dejectedly flopped on a chair opposite the couch. Purring loudly, Dopey jumped onto his lap and settled in. Gently rubbing the cat's chin, the pilot sighed, "I feel sorry for these guys."

Peter looked at him quizzically. "Why?"

"It took them two days to get used to Linda and me staying in the house." He continued to scratch Dopey's chin. "I guess they even hide from Cathy sometimes. Can you imagine what they're going to do when all those people from the Bureau enter this house?"

Leaning forward to pet Sneezy who had just sauntered into the room, Peter agreed: "Be pretty terrified, I imagine. But that can't be helped. I know firsthand that they do hide from strangers. When I first started coming here it took me a solid week before I finally won them over."

A hint of a smile briefly flitted across his face as the bittersweet memory of Cathy's words those first precious weeks flashed through his mind. "Love me, love my cats. That's my motto. If you don't love my cats then you don't love me."

Even the hint of a smile vanished, however, as reality once again set in. Tilting his head upward, he frowned at David. "What makes you think they hide from Cathy? In all the times I've been here, I've never seen them do that."

David seemed genuinely puzzled. "I don't understand. When Linda and I first got here, Cathy told us that when she arrived home that night, the cats had all disappeared." Looking down at Dopey, he smiled. "She found this poor little guy trapped behind the washer."

Peter rose so quickly from the couch that he frightened both Sneezy and Dopey. The cats scrambled from the room as if being chased by a pack of wild dogs. Rubbing his leg where Dopey's claws had dug in for traction, David scowled, "What did you do that for? You scared those poor cats half to death."

Grabbing his friend by the shirt collar, Peter practically dragged him out the back door. "Why didn't one of you tell me about the cats sooner?"

David shrugged. "We didn't think anything of it. It was no big deal. Why?"

Peter rolled his eyes, took a few steps, and then turned back to David. "Why? I'll tell you why. I think I know how the kidnappers have known our every move."

The expression on the novice agent's face changed from one of confusion to one of incredulity, his eyes growing enormous. "Geez, the cats, the house, you think whoever is behind Linda and Cathy's disappearance was in the house, don't you?" Peter merely nodded. Gazing into the house through the window, David slowly asked, "You think the house is bugged?"

"That would be my guess. But there's only one way to find out for sure." He pulled David's cell phone from the pilot's pocket and redialed headquarters. "I think the house is bugged. You better bring some equipment out here to check for sure." He handed the cell phone back to David. "When we are in the house, say nothing about this. Talk normally. If someone is listening, we don't want to tip him off too soon. Once we're sure there are bugs in the house, our people can fan out through the neighborhood. We should be able to pick up whoever is listening in without much trouble. This is a pretty quiet neighborhood. Unfamiliar cars or vans should be fairly easy to spot."

David swallowed hard. "You mean like the one we saw behind the vacant house the other day?"

Peter's voice was grim: "Exactly."

"Gotcha."

The Surveillance Van

After receiving Omar's phone call, Harold Wills decided to check things out for himself. Entering the van, he looked expectantly at Omar. "What's going on? Have the Feds arrived yet?"

"Naw, not yet."

Hearing only silence over the loud speakers, the attorney asked, "What are the men doing now?"

Omar shifted uneasily in his seat. "I'm not sure. They went outside a while ago and haven't returned."

The lawyer checked his watch. "Why did they go outside at this time of night?"

Omar shrugged. "Beats me."

Mr. Wills eyed his subordinate suspiciously. "Let me hear the tape of their last conversation."

When the lawyer heard the conversation about the cats, then about David being scratched, he grabbed the ex-con by the shoulder. "Get the van out of here now!!!"

"What?" asked a blinking Omar.

Wills rapidly crossed to the door. "You heard me! Do it now!! And never mind about trying to do it quietly. I've got to get my car out of here. We'll meet back at the warehouse."

"But what about the surveillance?" protested Omar, heading for the driver's seat.

"You idiot!! The others are new to the FBI so they didn't pick up on the cats, but Channing is not. Why do you think they're outside? Channing knows the house is bugged. It won't be long before they

begin searching the area. Now move it!!" With that his boss flew out
the door.

The Back Porch of Cathy's House

Peter, one hand on the doorknob, was just about to reenter the
house when two pairs of headlights snapped on in the woods across
the road. The men heard tires spinning as if desperately trying to gain
traction.

Peter ran for his truck, fumbling in his pocket for the keys. They
weren't there—he had left them in the house. Running for the back
door, the agent strained to see the fishtailing taillights now receding
out of sight. Realizing that by the time he retrieved his keys, the
owners of those lights would be long gone, he slowed to a walk.
"Damn!"

David raced up beside Peter. "How did they know we were on to
them?"

Peter stared in the direction of the vanished van as if trying to see
through the black wall of night. "They must have put two and two
together from our last conversation in the house."

"Now what do we do?"

Peter turned and stared at David as if seeing him for the first time.
"Nothing."

"Nothing? What do you mean nothing?"

"I mean we'll have to wait until daylight to see if we can figure out
exactly where *they* were located. Then we'll have to pray *they* left
some kind of clue as to who *they* are, or where *they* have gone."

"And if they have?" asked David hopefully.

"Then we'll have a chance of finding Cathy and Linda."

Continuing more cautiously now, David asked, "And if they
haven't?"

"Then we're back to square one." Peter re-entered the house,
letting the door slam behind him.

Chapter Thirty-Three

The Warehouse
Near Wilmington's International Airport

Anthony, Tony to his friends, sidled up to Timothy who sat slouched on a couch, watching an old western on the big screen television. Quietly, so as not to be overheard, the young man whispered, "I listened in on your conversation earlier. What they said is a bunch of B.S. I recognized one of the women they brought in here." Timothy would have sat up, but the young man who had become the self-appointed leader of the group placed a restraining hand on his shoulder. "Don't make any sudden moves. Pretend like you're still interested in the movie."

With his eyes focused on the television screen, Timothy asked, "Which one did you recognize?"

Answering out of the side of his mouth, Tony responded, "The taller one."

"Well, who is she?"

"You're not going to believe this, but she was a real good friend of the professor, if you get my drift."

Timothy abandoned any pretense of watching the television and stared incredulously at his comrade. "What? Are you sure?"

"I recognized her immediately. She was at the professor's office, not once but several times, when I stopped by to talk to him. I also saw her at his hotel a couple of times. They seemed real tight."

Timothy's brain felt mired in cotton candy. "But why would they tie her up? This doesn't make any sense."

Tony glanced around cautiously and shrugged. "With her tied up and the way the professor died, it does make you have to wonder." He glanced around again to make sure no one was watching them. "I'll just be glad when all this is over." Slowly, the self-appointed leader rose and stretched before ambling away.

Cathy's House

Randy, with the FBI team, walked into the screened-in porch where Peter and David sat drinking coffee. "We found listening devices in each of the phone receivers as well as in lamps in the living room and all the bedrooms. In addition, we discovered another one in the kitchen, and even one here on the porch." Randy sarcastically added, "About the only rooms they weren't interested in were the bathrooms."

"Is that supposed to be funny and make us feel better?" David snapped.

The team member quickly sobered. "Sorry about that."

Channing rose and patted the man on the shoulder, "Don't worry about it." Randy retreated back into the main part of the house. "It's not his fault, you know."

David stood up. "I know." The airline captain shook his arms as if trying to get circulation back into them. "It's just all this waiting and not knowing. It's driving me crazy." He stared out into the darkness and continued, talking to himself more than Peter: "I waited so long to find someone like Linda. I'd almost given up." His eyes had a far away look in them. "If something happens to her now, I honestly don't know what I'd do."

Peter shook his friend's shoulders, forcing an unfelt conviction into his tone: "We'll find her. Nothing is going to happen to either Linda or Cathy."

Straightening up, Sokol's eyes refocused. "Of course we will." He cleared his throat. "I better find Randy. I think I owe him an apology." With that, David entered the main part of the house.

Now it was Peter's turn to stare into the darkness. "Oh Cathy, David is not the only one who would be lost if something happened to the two of you."

The Mansion of Franklin Morse

Franklin Morse stepped into the cool autumn air, his briefcase and leather coat in hand. He turned to his security chief, Marcus. "You know exactly what to do tomorrow. As soon as the explosions are set off, eliminate Carl Austin and his pal, Omar. Make sure their remains are incinerated in that inferno. Then arrange for Harold Wills to drive his car into the Intracoastal Waterway. Make sure a suicide note is in a place where it will be easily found along with the papers connecting him to the warehouse and the boats. And whatever you do, make sure to get the key to the safety deposit box that he's stashed those pictures in!!"

His head of security stood at attention. "Yes, sir. It is all worked out."

Morse pointed his finger only a few inches from the man's face. "Make sure it is. Remember that you are to do this all yourself. I want no loose ends." He got into the back seat of a black limousine. "If you need me, I'll be at my home in Washington, surrounded by several members of Congress." He looked up at Marcus and smiled. "Who better to assure me of an ironclad alibi?"

The war veteran, watching the limousine's taillights recede down the driveway, gave a belated response to his boss: "Oh, I'll do everything as you say, all right. But those pictures in Harold Wills' safety deposit box, I think I'll keep those for myself. After all, Wills is right. A little insurance never hurts."

Chapter Thirty-Four

The Warehouse
Near Wilmington International Airport

Timothy pressed the knob on the side of his watch. The face lit up, indicating the time at 3:12 a.m. He rolled over and surveyed the room with his eyes. Everyone slept; the whole place was as silent as a tomb. Quietly, he slipped out from under his blanket and began to walk toward the bathroom.

Carl's eyes opened into slits as he watched Timothy's progress toward the bathroom. He lay there watching the boy, like an alligator lying by the side of a river pretending to nap while waiting for his next prey.

Timothy's hand rested on the handle of the bathroom door while he glanced back around the room. Seeing no one else stirring, he dropped his hand, detouring instead to the room holding the two women. The key was in the lock. Unlocking the door, he stealthily slid into the room. The student stared at the sleeping women, trying to decide what to do. Linda's eyes fluttered open, and upon spotting the intruder, opened wider. She prodded Cathy, who lay curled up in a ball next to her. Sitting up slowly, Cathy eyed the intruder suspiciously. "What do you want?"

Timothy stared at the woman. "Were you really a friend of the professor?"

"Yes," she replied dully.

"I'm sorry for your loss. The professor was a great guy. We all admired him. He was like a surrogate father to most of us here. His accident was such a terrible tragedy."

"That was no accident," Linda spat out.

Timothy squinted as he turned his attention to Linda. "What do you mean? Of course it was an accident."

Cathy eased out of bed, pulling the blanket around her shoulders. "No, it wasn't. Somebody murdered him and tried to make it look like an accident."

"Are you sure?"

"I'm afraid so."

"But that's not what we were told," Timothy insisted, now thoroughly confused.

Carefully, Cathy began to move toward the young man. "They lied to you. You have got to tell us what is going on here."

Timothy opened his mouth to respond when Harold Wills stepped into the room. "Is there a problem, Timothy? Carl was concerned and woke me when you came in here."

Confusion was clearly written across the young man's face. He pointed to Cathy. "She said the professor's death was no accident. How can that be?"

"Of course it was an accident. Can't you see she's just trying to trick you into helping them? Go back to bed now. You need to get some rest. Tonight you will complete the professor's greatest dream." He patted Tim's arm and escorted the young man out the door. Turning back to the women, the lawyer smiled, "Nice try, ladies."

Wills again locked the women in the room but this time took the key out of the lock and placed it on the desk near Carl. Indicating Timothy with his head, he whispered, "Don't let that kid out of your sight." Motioning toward the room confining the women, he added, "And make sure nobody else gets into that room. Understood?"

"You can count on it."

Timothy sat dejectedly on the side of his cot. Anthony rolled over and slowly opened his eyes, rising up on one elbow. "What are you doing up so early? Can't sleep because of tonight?"

Tim looked over at his new friend. "That's not it. I just paid a visit to those women they brought in."

Tony's brows shot up. "At this hour? Why?"

Tim leaned over to within a few inches of Tony's face. "Never mind that, just listen. According to his girlfriend, the professor's death was no accident. He was murdered."

Pushing Timothy away, Anthony swung his legs off the side of the bed. "Are you sure? Is she sure?"

"That's what she said."

"Maybe she was just trying to get you to help her?"

"I don't think so." He shook his head. "No, I definitely believe her."

Anthony sat silently and stared at the floor. Finally, Timothy broke the silence: "What are you thinking?"

"Remember right around the time the professor died, there was a news story about a guy's body being washed up on shore?"

"I knew him; I mean I'd seen him around. But what has he got to do with this?"

Tony bit the inside of his cheek. "He used to hang out with the professor, too. I don't believe in coincidences. Both die about the same time. Now you tell me that the professor may have been murdered. It makes me wonder."

Looking around nervously, Tim noticed Carl watching them. With his eyes still on Carl, he hissed, "Are you sure he was recruited by the professor?"

Noticing Carl's interest too, Tony slowly got back into bed. "I'm not positive, but it sure looked that way to me. Get back into bed. We're attracting too much attention."

Timothy did as he was told. "Well, what should we do?"

Tony closed his eyes. "Nothing for now. Let me think about it."

Lying on his cot and staring at the ceiling, Tim suddenly wished desperately to be home in his own bed. *Maybe if I go back to sleep, I'll wake up later and realize this was all just a horrible nightmare.*

Cathy's House

About one a.m., at Grayson's urging, David retired to the room he had shared with Linda. He lay on the bed, hugging Linda's pillow. It still smelled of the perfume she always wore. The scent was strangely comforting, so he finally drifted off to sleep.

Because agents dozed in the chairs and on the couches in the living room and family room, the FBI supervisor suggested that Peter stretch out in the master suite. Peter walked into the bedroom and shut the door. All the cats cautiously crawled out from under the bed. The tall agent gently sat on the floor and the cats encircled him, grateful for the sight of a familiar human. Petting each one in turn, Peter whispered, "Sorry, guys. I know you wish your Mama was here. So do I." He got up and lay on the bed, but sleep proved elusive.

Finally, at about 4:30, Peter rose and walked back through the living room and out onto the porch. Sitting in an old wooden rocker, the troubled agent rocked back and forth, back and forth. "Cathy, where are you?" he pleaded into the darkness that stretched like a curtain beyond the screen.

Chapter Thirty-Five

The Warehouse
Near Wilmington International Airport
Saturday Morning

Timothy never could go back to sleep. Tossing and turning, he finally rose at

5 a.m. *I can't just do nothing, I have to do something!* Looking over at Tony, who was snoring loudly, the young man scowled. *He won't be any help.* Next, the student glanced over at a sleeping Carl. Now was his chance. Tim slipped on his sandals and tiptoed toward the door to the women's room. It was again locked, but this time the key was not in the door. Desperate now, Timothy's eyes darted around the room, searching for the key. There it lay, on the desk next to Carl's sleeping form. He tiptoed over to the desk and leaned over the killer to reach the key. Just as he did so, Carl began to shift position. Tim froze. Luckily, the man never opened his eyes.

With key in hand, Tim practically ran back to the women's door and swung it open. Before the ladies could say anything, Tim put his hands to his lips. "Shshsh. I'm getting you out of here." The words had barely left his mouth when there was a hushed popping sound. For a moment, Tim's eyes widened in astonishment before the light in them faded into nothingness and he slumped to the floor, a spreading pool of blood soaking his shirt. Cathy quickly knelt down and felt for a pulse. Finding none, she slowly rose. The women grabbed on to one another. There, in the doorway, stood Cutthroat Carl with revolver in hand, maniacally grinning at them.

Wills appeared in the doorway. Staring down at the lifeless figure on the floor, he exploded, "What have you done? I only told you to keep an eye on him, not kill him."

Carl turned to Wills. "He was going to help them escape. I stopped him."

"You could have stopped him without killing him."

The murderer shrugged. "What difference does it make? He was going to die later today anyway."

The lawyer's patience was wearing thin. "The difference is, now we are minus one to drive the boats." He turned to within inches of Carl. "It will be up to you to find a replacement by tonight! Maybe you'd like to drive one of the boats yourself? Now get Omar in here, and the two of you clean up this mess."

Anthony rolled over and opened his eyes. Tim was not on his cot. *Maybe he's in the john,* he thought. It was then that he noticed the door to the women's room ajar. He was about to go and investigate when Harold Wills came storming out. Tony watched as Wills shook Omar awake, then saw the ex-con cross to the other room carrying the sheet that only a moment ago had covered him.

Anthony got up and used the bathroom. Exiting the facility, the young man collided with Omar, who was backing out of the office. Omar and Carl carried something wrapped in a sheet. Stepping back into the restroom's doorway to let them pass, he noticed that the collision had caused the sheet to unfold slightly, exposing the now ghostly white face of his young friend. Shock registered on Anthony's face as Carl and Omar hurried past. Wills rushed up and put his arm around Tony. Shaking his head in pretend sadness, he said, "Horrible, just horrible. The women tried to escape but Timothy stopped them. Unfortunately, one of them hit him over the head with a chair. Killed him instantly!"

Total disbelief was etched on Tony's face. There hadn't been any blood on Tim's face and there would have been if he had been hit in the head. Besides, from their earlier conversation, he knew that Tim would probably try to help the captives escape, not stop them. It was at that moment that the young man made up his mind. *It's time to get out. I'll take the women with me if I can. If not, I'll try to get help. We've been used. This is not what the professor wanted.* With a sudden clarity, Anthony knew the future and his dark eyes became like saucers. *We're all supposed to die tonight!!*

Chapter Thirty-Six

The Estate of Franklin Morse
North of Hampstead

Marcus walked leisurely down to Franklin Morse's cabin cruiser, floating near the end of the private pier attached to the property. The yacht was truly elegant, almost like a floating palace. It was not one of those modern sterile looking white jobs with tinted windows but a true classic with a teak deck polished to a dazzling shine.

Marcus looked back toward the house and felt a momentary sadness. This would probably be the last time he would see this house or walk these grounds. Last night he had decided that this was his final job for Franklin Morse. Drinking in the beauty of the surrounding grounds and impressive mansion, the head of security's eyes came to rest on the windows of the room that housed the models and his face sobered. *Morse is killing everyone off. Who's to say I won't be next? I can't take that chance. After I take care of Wills and the others, I am just going to continue down the Intracoastal Waterway and disappear.*

Marcus passed the luxurious cruiser and stepped aboard Morse's other, more modern yacht. "This will have to do," he murmured to himself. "The other would stand out in a crowd. This one won't." The ex-serviceman cast off and turned the boat toward Wrightsville Beach. The Intracoastal Waterway was filled with boats of every description: sailboats, fishing boats, yachts, small motorboats, even kayaks. Instead of docking at Wrightsville, however, he continued past and turned into a marina near Bradley Creek. He had enjoyed being able to borrow his boss's powerboats and sailboats on days and weekends off, *One of the better perks of the job,* and had rented space at the marina for just such occasions. *This is perfect, close enough for a speedy exit tonight, but not so close as to accidentally go up in the inferno.*

Marcus tied up at his dock space and stepped off the boat. He walked to his silver Miata, parked in the lot the night before. Placing the key in the car's ignition, he thought to himself, *This plan is not bad considering I just came up with it yesterday. If all goes well, it will look like the boat and I have gone up in smoke.*

Marcus drove to the warehouse, intending to ride shotgun over the rest of the operation, but changed his mind after spying Wills pull out of the lot. The head of security decided to tail him just in case the man went for the pictures. Staying a few car lengths behind, he followed Wills to the Bank of North & South Carolina and parked on the street under a magnolia tree. He observed Wills go into the bank then return a few minutes later carrying an envelope. Marcus's face lit up. "Bingo!" His hunch had paid off. Those had to be the pictures. An idea began to take shape in his mind as he followed Wills back to the warehouse. Making a "U" turn just before the warehouse parking lot, the security chief sped off.

Chapter Thirty-Seven

Cathy's House
Two Miles from Wrightsville Beach

Peter and David slept little. At the first sign of light the two men scoured the woods behind the house for any sign of the vehicles that had pulled away night the night before. Crumpled leaves and trampled pine straw indicated the spot where the van had been parked, but no other evidence remained. Searching behind the vacant house where they had spotted the van on Thanksgiving also turned up nothing. "If only we had searched the van when we passed here on Thursday, maybe none of this would have happened," sputtered David.

"We don't know that for sure. We don't even know if the van we saw here was involved in any way. The girls may have been right about it just being teenagers. We'll never know for sure. Just let it go."

The men walked back into the yard. Frustrated and angry, David began to chop wood while Peter decided to go for a jog. "Cathy, where are you? Cathy, where are you?" Peter kept repeating these words over and over as he ran, willing her to hear his thoughts and answer. The cell phone on his belt chirped. Breathless from the run, he stopped and answered it: "This is Channing."

"Peter, it's Emma." I'm afraid the bugs have turned up nothing. We can't trace them. I can tell you though that whoever was listening had to be pretty close to the house."

137

"Thanks for nothing. We already know where they were listening from."

"I'm sorry. Believe me we'll keep trying. We haven't given up hope. You shouldn't either."

Peter sighed. "I'm the one who is sorry. I know you are doing the best you can. What we need is a break." He signed off and walked dejectedly back to the house. He dreaded giving David this latest piece of news.

Peter had just walked up to David when another agent pulled up and got out. "We may have just caught a break. I've been showing Carl's picture to the local shops, and one of the girls at Java Joe's remembers him coming in on several occasions over the last few days."

"Did she remember anyone with him?" David asked eagerly.

"Well, no."

"What about the make of the car or even better, a license plate?" quizzed Peter.

"None of that, I'm afraid."

Peter exploded. "That's just great! We already knew about Carl. So, bottom line, we have nothing new. We're at another dead end." Peter turned and entered the house, letting the door slam.

The agent began to stammer, so David patted the man on the back. "It's not your fault. He's not angry with you. My friend's just frustrated, and if I know him, angry at himself for not having agents watch Cathy night and day." David patted the frustrated agent on the back, then turned and quietly followed Peter into the house.

Chapter Thirty-Eight

The Warehouse
Near Wilmington International Airport

At the sight of Timothy's lifeless body, the knot in Wills' stomach had tightened. Carl was totally out of control. Now they were short one driver for the boats, and the detonations had been carefully planned for six boats. Franklin Morse was not going to be happy about this at all. The industrialist would blame him. After all, he had chosen Carl Austin and had promised to keep the killer under control until the mission was over. Telling Austin to find another replacement without talking it over with the big man first might have been a mistake. Bringing someone new in at this late date would be taking a big risk. Harold Wills did not want that responsibility. The lawyer made up his mind. Morse had told him not to come to the house but had said nothing about phoning. Wills' hands shook as he dialed. It was picked up on the third ring. After first identifying himself, he asked to speak directly to Franklin Morse and was shocked to learn that Mr. Morse had left for Washington the night before. "When do you expect him back?"

"We do not expect Mr. Morse to return until next weekend," the voice on the other end replied.

"Did he leave any kind of message for me?"

The answer was a polite but firm, "No". Harold Wills hung up in a near panic. It had been his understanding that he would see Morse early tomorrow morning, collect the money, give Omar his share, and then head for Myrtle Beach to oversee the operation there. He had no intention of hanging around Wilmington for a whole week after tonight's disaster. Not to mention the fact that Omar might suspect him of keeping all the money for himself if he could not produce the subordinate's share right away.

The plan was unraveling. If not careful, he would be the one incriminated. *After all, I'm the one who made all the arrangements and recruited everyone who is involved; I've been the face that everyone's seen and the contact person from the very beginning.* A sense of foreboding filled the lawyer's mind. *Or has that been the plan all along? Has it always been Morse's intention for me to take the fall?* He shifted positions and stared into space. *No amount of money is worth this. And if I could escape, after such a monstrous act, what country worth living in would take me?* It was then that Harold Wills made his decision. *I've got to cut a deal with the FBI— it's my only chance. I'll show them the pictures of Franklin Morse's house.*

Harold Wills' Car

When Omar and Carl returned from disposing of Timothy's body, Wills told them to keep an eye on the rest of the students. "I've got an errand to run. I'll be back in a little while." Grabbing his car keys, the man practically sprinted to the car and started the engine. He decided to grab the pictures from his safety deposit box and go directly to the Cleveland woman's home. He knew the FBI was there. With luck, he would deal first with Channing. *Peter Channing and that pilot, David somebody, want their women back badly enough to put pressure on the higher ups to give me a better deal.* "It's worth a try anyway."

Wills retrieved the pictures and pulled out of the bank's parking lot. Glancing in his rearview mirror, he again noticed the silver Miata. He saw it first near the warehouse, then later at a stoplight. Now here it was again. The lawyer was being followed, but by whom? He needed to find out before proceeding anywhere else. Wills pulled onto the road and noted as the Miata again fell into line. This time, however, the attorney suddenly pulled into the next lane and slowed down. Because of the suddenness of the move and the heavy traffic in both lanes, the Miata was close enough for him to recognize the driver, Marcus. A sinking feeling engulfed him. Harold Wills had no choice but to return to the warehouse.

Chapter Thirty-Nine

The Mansion of Franklin Morse
North of Hampstead

After following Harold Wills back to the warehouse, Marcus made a beeline back to Franklin Morse's house. Heading straight for the room with the models, he spent the next hour playing with them. Finished, the models now depicted Morse's new industrial complex being built in an adjacent county. Rubbing hands together in satisfaction, he returned to the car and pulled out of the drive.

The Warehouse

A thick blanket of tension filled the air when Harold Wills returned to the warehouse. "What's going on?" he demanded.

"The boys are upset about Timothy," Carl replied nonchalantly.

"Did you tell them he died trying to keep the women from escaping?"

"They don't believe it," answered Omar.

Things just keep getting worse and worse. The whole plan is continuing to unravel! Aloud he asked, "Have the women had their breakfast?"

Carl shook his head in the negative. "Nah. Why feed them when we're just going to kill them later anyway?"

Harold Wills exploded! "You imbecile! Give me the key. I'll feed them myself." Grabbing food left over from the students' breakfast, Wills quickly made up two trays. Entering the women's room, he set the trays on the table and closed the door. Linda and Cathy looked warily at the trays, then at Harold Wills. "Look, I know you are upset by what happened this morning, but you really need to eat something."

Linda's voice was flat. "Why the pretend concern about us? It's pretty obvious you intend to kill us, too."

Cathy's voice dripped with sarcasm. "Well, maybe not you personally, but definitely that gorilla out there in the Panama hat."

Harold Wills glanced behind him to be sure Carl hadn't opened the door. "Not if I can help it." Leaning close to Cathy, he asked, "Is Peter Channing an honorable man?"

Cathy pushed the man away. Caught off guard by the question, she eyed the man uncertainly. "What kind of crazy question is that? Look, is this some kind of weird mind game you are trying to play?" She slid past Wills and crossed the room.

Following her, the lawyer continued, "I'm serious. Look, I want to put an end to this, but I need to know whom I can trust."

Cathy stared at him for a moment. "If you are serious, then the answer to your question is yes, Peter Channing is an honorable man."

"Good, then I will go and get him. With luck, this should all be over in a matter of a few hours."

Linda stepped forward. "Why not take us with you?"

"No! Carl might get suspicious. Then there's no telling what he'd do! You are right about him, Ms. Cleveland. He is a gorilla. No, it's better I go and bring back help." He looked at the still uneaten food. "You'd better eat something quick so I can get out of here."

After the women had finished their breakfasts, Wills gathered up the trays and exited the room. He was trying to balance the trays with one hand and lock the door with the other when a hand took the key out of his. "Here, let me help you with that." Harold Wills turned to find Marcus directly behind him, calmly sipping a bottle of water.

The lawyer's jaw dropped. "What are you doing here?"

Marcus eyed the envelope protruding from Wills' inside jacket pocket. "Our mutual employer thought I should personally oversee the final preparations." Leaning past Harold to lock the door, Marcus accidentally spilled water all over Harold Wills. Putting the bottle and the key down, Marcus quickly took the trays from Harold and helped him remove his jacket. "I'm sorry about that. You're soaked. You'd better go dry yourself off before you get chilled. You wouldn't want to be sick for tonight's festivities, now would you?"

Nervous about leaving his jacket yet not wanting to draw attention to it, Wills did as told. Returning quickly, he was gratified to see the envelope still safely secure in the jacket pocket. The wet jacket gave him an idea. Picking the jacket up, he turned to Marcus, "This jacket water spots, so if you don't mind, I want to take it to the cleaners. I'll need it for tonight. I know a dry cleaner that boasts of cleaning in only a few hours. If I go now, it should be done in time."

Marcus smiled. "Sure, you go right ahead. I'll keep an eye on things."

Chapter Forty

Harold Wills pulled into Cathy Cleveland's driveway. Before he had gone ten feet up the drive, a man in a dark suit and sunglasses stopped him. Wills rolled his window down. "What business do you have here?" the man demanded.

"I'm here to see Peter Channing."

The man in the sunglasses eyed Wills suspiciously. "What do you want with Peter Channing?"

"It's about his lady friend Cathy Cleveland."

The man in the dark glasses straightened up and whispered something into a walkie-talkie, and without saying another word, signaled Wills to proceed the rest of the way up toward the brick structure. By the time Harold pulled next to the house, Peter Channing and David Sokol were standing on the porch. "This could be the break we've been waiting for," whispered David excitedly.

Peter urged more caution: "Don't get your hopes up just yet."

Before the lawyer could step out of his car, another man in dark glasses appeared with gun drawn. "Please step out of the car and place your hands on the roof." The attorney complied. The man ran his hands over Wills' clothes. Assured that the stranger carried no concealed weapon, he allowed Wills to slowly turn around. "Go ahead!" he commanded, indicating the house.

Peter Channing watched the stranger approach the porch. Before he reached the steps, Peter blocked his path. "What do you know about Cathy Cleveland?"

Harold Wills took a deep breath. *This is it,* he thought. *There is no turning back now.* "I know where she and the other woman are and what is going on."

Channing looked at Sokol before stepping back and opening the door. "Come in."

Once the three men were seated in the living room, the airline captain exploded, "Where are they?"

The lawyer was not prepared for the sudden outburst. "Not so fast."

The veteran agent gazed impassively at Wills. "Of course. Let me guess. You want to make a deal."

"Of course."

David jumped out of his chair. "Time is wasting. I asked you, where are they? Every minute we waste could be Linda's last."

Wills ignored the outburst and, instead, focused attention on Peter. "The women are safe for the time being. I promise you that. But the longer you wait, the less they will be."

The agent drummed his fingers on the chair's arm. "Very well, I'll need to get my supervisor."

Two hours later, with a promise of immunity from prosecution and placement in the witness protection program in exchange for his testimony, Harold Wills began his story. No one in the room, except the lawyer turned criminal, said anything for a solid hour. When he finished, a low whistle came out of the pilot's throat. Channing looked at Wills. "That is a pretty fantastic story if it is true. Franklin Morse is a well-known and well-respected member of this community, as well as being very influential in Washington. You said you had proof. Now would be a good time to show us that proof."

The man removed the envelope containing the pictures from his jacket pocket and handed them to the agent. Opening the envelope

146

and looking through the pictures, Peter's face registered first astonishment and then anger. "Is this some kind of a sick joke?" Standing up, the FBI agent threw the pictures on the coffee table. Visible to all in the room were pictures of scantily dressed women in provocative poses. Not one was of Franklin Morse's property or the room with the construction models.

"I don't understand," Wills mumbled, quickly leafing through the pornographic pictures. Then the recollection of the spilled water flashed through his mind. "Wait a minute." He desperately grabbed Channing by the shirtsleeve. "He must have known I was going to talk so he switched the pictures."

The veteran agent sat back down. "Who switched the pictures?"

"Marcus, Franklin Morse's security chief. I saw him following me when I got the pictures out of my safety deposit box. Later, he showed up at the warehouse and spilled water all over me. I was only gone a minute or two to dry off, but that must have been enough time for him to switch the pictures." Looking around the room, Wills sensed the doubt and disbelief. "Wait a minute. I've still got the camera in my glove compartment. Plug it into your computer and see for yourselves."

Wills began to head for the door when two agents blocked his path. He turned to the others and suggested, "Then you go get the camera."

Emma Grayson nodded her head at the two agents nearest the door and they disappeared, only to return a minute later with the camera. The camera was quickly plugged into the FBI laptop computer on the dining room table. All backs were bent over and all eyes glued on the monitor as the images came into focus. The FBI supervisor slowly straightened up and turned burning eyes on Harold Wills. "Mr. Wills, I don't know what your game is, or if you simply get some perverse pleasure in wasting our time, but your time here is up." Turning to another agent she continued, "Please escort this man to his car."

Wills wrestled away from the man's grip and muscled his way past the gawking agents. There on the screen, in full color, were the same scantily clad women in the same provocative poses as in the pictures now strewn all over the coffee table. "Marcus must have gotten to the camera too. You've got to believe me!" Wills pleaded as he looked around the room into disbelieving eyes. "Don't you want to save your women? Go to the warehouse. They are there and so are the young students. I swear."

Peter and David stood up. Harold Wills moved as if to go with them. "You stay here!" Peter commanded. "We'll check out the warehouse."

Emma Grayson broke in. "Very well, but we'll send several agents."

Her subordinate begged to let the two of them first go alone. "If too many agents go, gunfire will probably erupt and the women might get caught in the crossfire. Let us see what's going on and if there is any truth to what this man says. If there is, we'll holler for back up. I promise."

The FBI supervisor reluctantly agreed. "All right. But if what this man says is true, and, at this point, I'm definitely not saying that I believe him, then the mission must come first. Do you understand me?"

Peter Channing stared into his superior's unblinking eyes and knew all too well what she meant. The women would be sacrificed if needed to stop Franklin Morse's diabolical plot. Peter nodded.

Stomping down the back steps, he muttered, "Over my dead body they will be!!!"

The Warehouse

Because of the holiday traffic, it took Peter and David forty-five minutes to reach the warehouse. They parked the car in the parking lot across the street and faced the warehouse. "Seems awfully quiet to me," David said, scratching his head.

Peter tugged on his lower lip with his fingers. "Yeah. Too quiet. Let's go." They got out of the car and crossed the street. "Do you have your cell phone?" David nodded. "Set it on vibrate." The pilot did so. "You cover the front. I'll see if there's another entrance around back." Both men pulled out their revolvers. "Wait for me to call before you enter."

Channing located the back entrance. With revolver at the ready, he called his partner. Both men burst into the warehouse simultaneously only to find it completely empty. "Check the offices!"

David Sokol ran recklessly first to one office, then the other.

Peter called out after him. "Find anything?"

"Nothing!" The airline pilot walked dejectedly back into the main area.

Slamming his weapon against the top of the empty metal desk, the veteran hissed, "We've been had! Let's get out of here."

The men sprinted back to the car. Putting the car in gear and rolling forward even before the front doors closed, Peter peeled out of the parking lot, the speedometer reading sixty before finally backing down to the legal forty-five. Neither man spoke for a long time. Finally, David broke the silence: "What do you think?"

Peter's expression was grim. "Either Harold Wills is a flat-out liar, or they anticipated our coming and cleared out before we had time to get here." When the FBI agent finished speaking, he opened his cell phone and called Emma Grayson. "I need a search warrant."

Cathy's House

Peter had barely turned off the engine when David leaped out of the car and ran into the house. Grabbing Wills by the shirt collar, hoisting him to his feet, and shaking him violently, the would-be bridegroom shouted, "They weren't there!!!"

Several agents had to pull the distraught pilot away from a trembling Harold Wills, who collapsed into a chair. "I swear to you I'm telling the truth!"

Peter Channing walked into the room and spoke barely above a whisper. "Mr. Wills, you are going to accompany us to Franklin Morse's house. You are going to show us the room where the models are located. And I swear to you that if you have been wasting our time and lying to us, you are going to regret the moment you walked into this house." He lifted Harold Wills up by the back of his neck and marched him out the door.

Before the agent could pull out, his superior hurried up to the car window and rapped on it. When Peter rolled it down, Emma Grayson thrust a paper into his hand. "You'll need this. Don't do anything stupid! I don't care what Ms. Cleveland is to you. You are still an agent of the FBI. I expect you to act like one." She pointed toward David Sokol. "And for heaven's sake, keep that one under control!"

The Mansion of Franklin Morse

An hour later Channing parked in front of Franklin Morse's southern mansion. With Harold Wills sandwiched between the two men, Peter rang the bell. The butler answered the door: "May I help you?"

The agent gave him the search warrant and asked to see Franklin Morse. The butler barely glanced at the document. "Mr. Morse is away on business and will not return until the end of the week."

"What about the head of security? I want to talk to him," pressed Peter.

A man who Harold Wills had never seen before came to the door, and the butler handed him the warrant. "You wanted to see me?" the man said as he read the search warrant.

"You're not head of security," Harold shouted. "Where's Marcus?"

"Oh, but I am head of security. Who is Marcus?"

"I don't know Marcus's last name, but he is head of security for Morse Industries." Harold Wills was in a full-blown panic now.

"I'm afraid you have been misinformed." Turning to Peter, the unidentified man inquired, "May I ask what this is all about?"

"What's your name?" demanded David.

"Ben Denton."

"Mr. Denton, how long have you been head of security for Morse Industries?" asked Peter, casting a warning look at his friend.

"About five years."

'And I suppose you can prove that?" cut in David, ignoring Peter's face.

Ben Denton paused for a moment. "Why yes, yes I can. I can show you my pay stubs if you like. Or you can ask any of the staff." He inclined his head toward the butler who nodded in the affirmative.

The veteran agent sounded annoyed. "Never mind. We want to look at some of your downstairs rooms, if you don't mind."

Indicating the warrant in his hand, Denton replied, "With this, obviously I don't have much choice."

The two agents pushed Harold Wills ahead of them. "Show us the room."

"It may be locked. It was the day I took the pictures."

Peter glanced back at Denton. "I'm sure the head of security has a key if it is."

Ben Denton remained standing at the front door with the butler. "The rooms on this floor are never locked."

The lawyer opened the door. Glancing at the models, he sighed with relief. "Here they are."

The men walked over to the models and stared. The airline captain's contempt was almost palpable. "Mr. Wills, please come over here and read the labels on these models."

Reading from the labels, Harold Wills' face fell. The models were all legitimate renderings of Franklin Morse's empire. He faced the FBI agents. "But they were here, I swear it!"

Leading the entourage back to the front door, Channing stopped and turned toward the butler. "One more thing." Pointing to Harold Wills he asked, "Have you ever seen this man before?"

The butler tilted his head to one side as he studied Harold Wills. "I think he may have been a guest at one of Mr. Morse's parties about a month ago."

"But that's the only time you've seen him?" The butler nodded. "You're sure?"

"Quite sure, sir." With that the butler held the door until the men exited, then quietly closed it.

The butler looked nervously at Ben Denton. "How did we do?"

Franklin Morse pulled off his disguise. "Perfectly. Now call the airport. I must get back to Washington before I'm missed."

The Driveway in front of the Mansion

Peter drummed his fingers on the steering wheel as the three men sat in the car in Morse's driveway. "Now what?" asked a frustrated David.

"What about the boats?" Harold Wills piped up from the back seat.

Peter stared at Harold Wills through the rear view mirror. "Do you know where they all are?"

The frightened lawyer reached into his wallet and pulled out a slip of paper. "Yes, I have all that information right here."

"Well, what are we waiting for? Let's go!" shouted David impatiently.

After grabbing the sheet from the attorney, the veteran agent called his superior and relayed the information. "Send agents to each of the following sites. We'll take the marinas by the bridge that leads to Wrightsville Beach."

A Marina at Wrightsville Beach

Because of the festivities, traffic was heavier than usual around the beach. Peter drove carefully, weaving in and out, and stopping for pedestrians that crossed the street anywhere they pleased. He finally found a place to park across the street from the waterway. Walking among the vessels tied to the docks, the trio found the first boat. Jumping on board, the two agents searched the vessel from one end to the other while Wills waited nervously on deck. They found nothing. Quickly retracing their steps, they found another boat on the list. This time it was a sailboat. The three were about to board, when a man and a woman came up from the galley below. "What do you thing you're doing?" demanded the man.

Peter looked at Wills. "Do you know these people?"

Harold stared at the couple and slowly shook his head no.

The two agents flashed their badges toward the couple. "We have reason to believe there may be explosives aboard your boat and would like permission to search it. We can get a search warrant if we have to, but that would take time."

The woman clung to her husband's arm. "Explosives?"

The man looked at the badges, then at the agents. "By all means, come aboard. If there are explosives here, we'd like to know."

Again the men searched, but to no avail. They radioed the other units, but all the responses were the same. The boats were all where Harold Wills said they would be, but none had explosives on board. Peter apologized to the couple as the group left the sailboat.

Harold Wills was frantic now. "But there were supposed to be explosives on all those boats, I tell you!!"

David grabbed Harold by one elbow and Peter did the same to the other. They marched Harold to the car and practically threw him into the back seat. The three men sat in the car, not saying a word for five minutes. Peter drummed his fingers on the steering wheel. Finally, David broke the silence: "So what do you think?"

Peter turned slowly to face his comrade and gestured toward the back seat. "I think either our friend here is a compulsive liar or they suspected he had turned and cleaned up any evidence."

"I'm not lying!" Harold Wills grabbed the front seat with both hands as he shouted from the backseat.

David shoved the desperate man backwards into the second seat. Peter turned all the way around to face the lawyer, staring into Harold Wills' eyes as if trying to see into his soul. Sensing the truth, the twenty-five year veteran of the FBI shrugged and said, "I believe you."

"So where does that leave us?" inquired a totally frustrated Captain David Sokol.

Gunning the engine as he started the car, an equally frustrated Peter Channing replied, "Back to square one." Putting the car in gear, he continued, "I guess we have no choice but to go back to Cathy's house and see if we've somehow missed something."

"What about me?" whispered Harold Wills.

"You are definitely staying with us!" both men replied in unison.

Chapter Forty-One

The Warehouse
Near Wilmington International Airport

As soon as Harold Wills left the warehouse, Marcus began to bark orders. He contacted Franklin Morse and knew that the great man himself was already airborne and on his way back. The security chief had to admire the man for the entire contingency plan that had been put in place for just such an emergency. Identical boats were already being substituted for the boats loaded with explosives. The original boats along with their young pilots were now safely hidden away in a new location. Huge semis, with drivers loyal to Franklin Morse, arrived shortly after Harold Wills drove off, and all the contents of the warehouse were already loaded into them. All that remained were the women.

Marcus unlocked the door to their prison. Cathy and Linda backed up as the door swung open. "Who are you?" asked Linda, untying the scarf from around her neck and dropping it behind her.

Grabbing each one roughly by the shoulder, Marcus shoved them out the door. "Sorry ladies, but there is no time for pleasantries." He paused only long enough to pick up Linda's scarf. Focusing ice-cold eyes onto the petite woman, the ex-soldier continued, "Nice try. In the military I was taught to always know my enemy. You both made quite a splash in the headlines last summer. I know all about how the discovery of your scarf gave the FBI the clue they needed to break the case. Sorry. Not this time." Marcus tied the women up and made them lie down in the back of a white minivan borrowed from the Franklin Morse estate. He drove directly to the marina near Bradley Creek. The security chief decided to hide the women temporarily in the boat he planned to use for his own escape. *A little more insurance,* Marcus thought to himself. *Not even Franklin Morse himself knows about this, let alone Omar or Carl.*

Mid-afternoon before the Flotilla

Marcus waited to unload his cargo until some of the other sailors finished their last-minute decorations for the flotilla, now only four hours away.

With the women stashed in the storage room, Marcus walked leisurely up the gangway. Touching the envelope containing Harold Wills' pictures hidden securely inside his shirt, he finally began to relax. *Time to enjoy the festivities until tonight's big finale.*

Chapter Forty-Two

Cathy's House
Two Miles from Wrightsville Beach
Late Afternoon before the Flotilla

Peter pulled into Cathy's drive, which was quickly filling with cars from the units that had checked out the other boats. Slamming the door, the three men strode into the living room. "Everyone please take a seat," commanded the FBI supervisor. "You have searched the boats, the warehouse, and Franklin Morse's house and have so far come up empty. If what Harold Wills has told us is indeed the truth, and the consensus is that we do believe him, we are running out of time. Any suggestions on where we go from here?" She acknowledged Channing's raised hand: "Go ahead."

"We should keep an eye on those boats. Obviously, if Wills is telling the truth, the boats we checked out have to be decoys. Morse's friends are going to have to swap them for the real ones sooner or later."

Grayson agreed. "Done." The superior gave word to send agents back to the boats.

"I also think that David and I should take Mr. Wills and mingle with the crowds at Wrightsville Beach. He might be able to spot this Marcus character or maybe some of the students."

"Agreed."

Another agent raised his hand. "What about canceling the flotilla and evacuating Wrightsville Beach?"

"That option was examined and scratched, at least for now. The higher-ups feel that since we don't have any real proof, only this man's word," she pointed to Harold Wills, "we could be starting a panic for nothing. Besides, at this late date, it would be almost impossible to get everyone off the island and away from the waterway in time." Emma Grayson looked around the room.

"Anything else?"

When no one else responded, she concluded, "Then I suggest you grab something to eat and let's get on with it. It's going to be a long afternoon and, if we can't find the boats rigged with explosives in time, an even longer night."

One of the unit members had just finished handing out sandwiches and bottles of water when the phone rang. The supervisor answered it and then bolted upright. "What?" she practically yelled into the phone. Her voice quieted and she continued: "Yes, I understand. Well, keep looking. Get some choppers in the air to help. And for heaven's sake, keep me posted." She hung up and looked around the room. "The units that went to keep an eye on the boats have just reported in. They are all gone. Vanished."

Peter dropped his sandwich into the trash. "Let's go!"

David swallowed his last bite. "Right behind you." He grabbed Wills by the shirtsleeve. "You, too."

Chapter Forty-Three

The women examined their makeshift prison. "How considerate of him to leave us with a portable toilet," commented Linda dryly.

"Yeah, we even have a sink for water. Of course, with our hands tied behind us, it doesn't do much good. We need to take inventory of what's in here. We just might be able to use something."

As the two searched their environment, Linda glanced over at her friend. "I sure would like to know what this is all about, wouldn't you?"

"You got that right." Suddenly her face lit up. "I think I've found something."

Linda crossed to her friend. "What is it?"

"Some kind of machinery lubricant. Probably used on the marine engine."

So what good is that going to do us?"

"Remember when I tried your engagement ring on and it got stuck on my finger?"

"Yeah, so?"

"Remember how I got it off?"

Linda nodded. "You used your hand lotion." Frustrated now, Linda frowned at her friend, "I repeat my question. So?"

"We use the same principle to slip the ropes off our wrists, only we use this lubricant instead of lotion. Get it?"

"Oh, I get it all right. But even if we can get our hands free, what good will it do? The door is locked. What do you propose we do about that?"

Cathy sighed. "First things first. First our hands, after that we'll deal with the door."

"I have one more question."

"What's that?"

Linda looked at the can. "With our hands tied behind us, how do we get the lid off?"

Cathy grinned at her friend. "With your knees to hold the can, your eyes to tell me what to do, and my hands to twist the cap."

"You've got to be kidding!"

"Nope."

Fifteen minutes later, rubbing their now raw wrists made sore by the chafing of the ropes, they faced the next problem, the locked cabin door. The women searched the shelves in vain for something heavy enough to pound against it. There was nothing strong enough to dislodge the door.

Next they searched around the rope coiled in the far corner of the room. Just as they were about to give up, there it was, hidden under the yards of rope, a relatively small yet heavy spare anchor. It took both women to lift it. Together they rammed the door again and again. Ten minutes later the door still hadn't given way. Panting from near exhaustion and in total desperation, they gave one final mighty effort. Backing up to the wall opposite the door and yelling at the top of their lungs, the two lunged headlong at full speed, the anchor firmly planted in front of them like a battering ram. The women hit the door with all the strength left in them. Tumbling through the doorway, their momentum crashing them into the opposite wall, they collapsed on top of each other in a heap. Lying there for a full two minutes trying to catch their breath, Linda finally rolled off Cathy and the two checked themselves for broken bones. The computer analyst had a goose egg forming where her head had collided with Cathy's. The college instructor's right forearm was turning purple where it had connected with the wall. But all that seemed unimportant now. They were free.

Grabbing Cathy by the hand, Linda yelled, "Let's get out of here."

The time was now 5:25—one hour and five minutes before the start of the flotilla.

Chapter Forty-Four

Carl and Omar hustled the young men out of the warehouse and into a nondescript olive green minivan. From the warehouse they traveled to a private marina just to the north of Wrightsville Beach. There, in a row, sat boats identical to their own, but with different names. "Your boats, gentlemen," grinned Carl.

Tony appeared confused. "That's not mine. Mine is called 'The Minerva'."

"Same boat, we just changed the name," added Omar.

"But what about the flotilla entry forms?" asked Bobby Bristol, one of the twins.

"Not to worry. These are the actual names of the boats, so the registry is all proper. Boats with those other names are also registered for the flotilla. It's just a little added safeguard," a very pleased Carl responded.

Tony looked around desperately. He felt time for himself and the others running out. "Where's Mr. Wills? I want to talk to him."

Omar shifted uneasily, so Carl quickly cut in. "You don't want to bother Mr. Wills. He's busy seeing to the last-minute details. Why don't you tell me what's on your mind?"

Tony shrank back. "Never mind. It's not that important."

"Well then, you gentlemen should check your boats," Cutthroat Carl smirked. "Oh, and make sure all your holiday lights are working. We wouldn't want to disappoint the crowds, now would we?"

The killer turned to the ex-con. "Keep an eye on them. We passed a fast food joint on the way up here. I'm going back to get some lunch." Gesturing toward the boys, he added, "We wouldn't want them to die on empty stomachs, now would we?"

"What's the plan for us?"

"As soon as the boys leave the docks, we'll hot foot it back down to Wrightsville Beach. By the time they cruise on down there. We'll be in position." That familiar crazy glazed gleam emanated from Carl's eyes once again as he smacked his lips. "It's just a matter of time, now."

"What about Marcus?"

"He'll meet us on the side road that runs parallel to the Intracoastal Waterway. You know the one to the left, just before you cross over the Wrightsville Beach Bridge. He'll have the women with him." After a moment's pause, the killer took out his knife and gingerly touched the blade. He sneered. "Fitting don't you think?"

"How do you mean?"

He continued to fidget with the knife. "Well, after all, we are going to help them cross over another bridge tonight."

What other bridge?"

"The bridge to the great beyond."

Omar could still hear the echo of maniacal laughter as his partner pulled out of the lot.

Chapter Forty-Five

The Georgetown Townhouse of Franklin Morse
Outside Washington, D.C.
Late Saturday Afternoon

At precisely 5:00 Franklin Morse stood in the foyer of his Georgetown townhouse, greeting his thirty dinner guests. Congressmen and women and their spouses or significant others, as well as a few diplomats from various embassies, made up the dinner-party roster. He wanted to be surrounded by unimpeachable witnesses when the news broke about the tragedy that was about to befall his beloved hometown of Wilmington. He glanced unobtrusively at his watch before shaking the hand of the diplomat from France. *It won't be long now.* "Margaret, may I say you look spectacular tonight," The business tycoon, looking dashing in a dark blue dinner jacket, gushed as he greeted another guest from Great Britain. The woman blushed and giggled like a teenager before moving on.

At 5:30 a servant entered the living room, where the guests were enjoying cocktails, and announced that dinner was served. As the guests moved toward the dining room, Franklin Morse whispered to one of his trusted aides, "Let me know as soon as the news breaks."

Chapter Forty-Six

Wrightsville Beach
Just East of Wilmington

Peter Channing, David Sokol, and Harold Wills walked among the throngs that vied for spots to sit or stand to watch the flotilla. Hundreds of people and cars packed the Intracoastal Waterway embankments. Countless others partied on their boats or prepared to get underway.

At exactly 5:30 Peter's cell phone rang. He flipped it open. "Peter Channing."

"Peter, it's Cathy!"

"Cathy?" At the utterance of her name, David made a grab for the phone, but Peter swept David's hand away with his arm. "Cathy, are you all right? Where are you?"

"Ask her about Linda," David shouted.

Cathy could hear the pilot in the background. "Tell David Linda's fine. We're at a marina near Bradley Creek."

"Stay there. We'll be right over to pick you up!"

"No! We can't stay here. It's not safe. We were being held on a boat. We managed to escape, but he might come back. I'll tell you what. There's a cemetery near here. I can't remember the name, but you know which one I mean?"

"Yeah, the one between the marina and Greeneville Loop Road."

"We'll meet you there. Linda and I will stay hidden until I see you pull in."

Peter was about to agree, but changed his mind. "No, wait. We're at the beach, and with this crowd it would take us too long to get there and back. Emma Grayson is at your house. I'll call and have her send agents to pick you up and bring you both here."

"Why bring us to the beach? What's going on?"

"We'll fill you both in when you get here, I promise." Peter hit the end button and dialed Cathy's house, still command headquarters. As soon as he finished filling his superior in, two agents were dispatched to pick up the women and deliver them directly to the waiting men.

"Peter, you do realize we are running out of time? We now have less than one hour until the flotilla starts." David's words sank in.

"I know. I know." Peter's euphoria at the rescue was short lived, replaced instead by the reality of the impending disaster.

Chapter Forty-Seven

Wrightsville Beach
Just East of Wilmington

Marcus strolled among the vendors at the little fair at Wrightsville Beach Park, an event that preceded the Flotilla. Earlier he had finished making final preparations to eliminate all those involved and make his disappearance look like he had been consumed by the inferno along with everyone else. The soon-to-be ex-security chief rubbed his hands together in anticipation. *Yes, it's going to be a great night!* He checked his watch. It was not quite 5:15. "Time to pick up the women," he muttered. An older woman standing nearby heard his comment and gave him a disgusted look. Marcus decided to play along and leered openly at her. She looked aghast and scurried away.

Pulling into the marina near Bradley Creek at 5:30 and crossing directly to Franklin Morse's cabin cruiser, Marcus went below deck, only to reappear a minute later. The women were gone! "Damn!" he cursed, "Not now!" Quickly grabbing the binoculars that hung on the ship's console, he scanned the surrounding area for any sign of them. *Nothing!!* Keeping the binoculars around his neck, the head of security ran for his car. He would leave the minivan here and take the Miata instead. *I've got to get out of here. The Miata is fast and maneuverable. If the women are free, it will only be a matter of time before agents swarm this vessel.* Marcus knew the boat and the minivan could be tied to Franklin Morse. *Morse can always claim that they were stolen. Besides, he has enough lawyers. They can get the big man out of just about anything!*

The car's wheels spun as the security chief gunned the engine, turning from the marina parking lot onto Oleander Drive. "Slow down", he commanded himself. "I don't want to get pulled over now." His mind reeled. He had to rethink the plan. The boat was no longer his ticket out of town. *When this is all over, I'll just get in the Miata and drive south to Florida.* The security chief nodded in satisfaction. *With luck, by tomorrow night I can catch a flight out of Miami. Rio should be beautiful this time of year!*

It was exactly 5:50 when Marcus pulled onto the side road that ran parallel to the Intracoastal Waterway. It was here that he was to meet Carl and Omar. Parking under the trees and far enough down so as not to be noticed by the heavy traffic crossing over the Wrightsville Beach Bridge, the ex-soldier opened the glove compartment and pulled out a gun. Slowly, he attached a silencer onto the barrel.

Chapter Forty-Eight

Wrightsville Beach
Just East of Wilmington

Even before the nondescript sedan came to a complete stop, Linda and Cathy opened their car doors. Both women leaped out and into the waiting arms of David and Peter. David smothered his bride-to-be with kisses, oblivious to the crowd of onlookers. Peter, on the other hand, merely hugged Cathy, trying to keep one eye on Harold Wills. As the time for the flotilla drew closer and closer, he worried Wills might suddenly change his mind and bolt.

When Peter finally released Cathy, she demanded, "What is going on? Why are you here?" Noticing Harold Wills, she added, "And why is he with you?"

Hearing Cathy's questions, Linda pulled away from David. "Yeah, what is going on?"

Leading the women to a quieter spot, Peter proceeded to bring both up to speed. Linda looked incredulous, but Cathy seemed genuinely sad. "I just can't believe that the same John Marley I knew would have anything to do with this."

"I'm afraid it's true," Harold Wills finally spoke. "He did all the recruiting for us."

"But why? Did he ever tell you that?"

"The same as the rest of us: greed."

"Why was he killed?" asked Linda.

"The Bureau was getting too close, putting things together. Franklin Morse likes to make sure there are no loose ends or trails that can be followed."

Cathy walked away and stared out at the water. Shivering, she was suddenly aware of a presence beside her. Peter put a protective arm around her. "Cold?"

Cathy looked up at him and shook her head, turning back to the water. "Not really. I'm just having a hard time wrapping my mind around the fact that someone I liked and genuinely admired was nothing but a greedy criminal who had no compunction about putting hundreds, if not thousands of people in harm's way."

Peter looked down at Cathy and spoke quietly, "He may have been that, but from what you told me he was also an amazing teacher, capable of motivating young minds to explore the universe around them."

Returning his look, Cathy gave him half a smile. "Thank you for saying that." Glancing back at the others, she shook off her self-pity. "Come on. We've got to find those boats."

It was now 6:00, thirty minutes to the start of the flotilla.

Chapter Forty-Nine

A Private Marina
A Few Miles North of Wrightsville Beach

At precisely 5:40 Carl Austin instructed the young men to cast off. "We want you in position when the parade starts, but not too much beforehand." The five boats slowly pulled away from their moorings and began their journey down the waterway. Once the vessels were well on their way, Carl turned to Omar. "Let's get out of here." The men climbed into the minivan and headed for Wrightsville Beach.

"Whatever happened about the sixth boat?" asked Omar.

"They don't need it. Five will work just fine."

"What about the bridge?"

"Look under the tarp in the back." Omar eased his way into the back of the van and removed the tarp. There lay enough explosives to level a five-story building. "I figured I'd park the van under the bridge with the women inside and detonate it by remote control. "Bye-bye bridge and bye-bye women, but not before I phone Channing and tell him where they are. I wouldn't want him to miss the show!"

The Side Road Near the Wrightsville Beach Bridge

It was 5:58 when the white minivan pulled behind the silver Miata. Marcus climbed out of his vehicle and approached the van. "Where are the women?" demanded Carl.

"Change of plans." The scowl on Carl's face died with him as a bullet entered his brain, right between his eyes. Too late, Omar tried to pull a gun from his waistband. A bullet entered his heart and he was dead before his head hit the dashboard. Marcus returned to the little sports car, calmly unscrewed the silencer from the front of the gun, and placed both back in the glove compartment. Not since Iraq had he done any actual killing. On Franklin Morse's command, he had occasionally arranged for the disappearance of some of his boss's competitors. The ex-GI shrugged. Funny how easy it is to slip back into old patterns. When this is all over, maybe I should become a mercenary.

Pulling away from the crime scene, the security chief glanced in his rearview mirror. "Two of your problems have now been taken care of, Mr. Morse." He drove onto Airlie Drive and parked along the side of the road behind a long line of vehicles. The killer got out and began to walk toward his destiny.

The security chief needed to get into position to detonate the boats. Absorbed in his own thoughts, he nearly missed seeing Harold Wills and the two women. Quickly Marcus ducked behind a parked car and watched the group pass. *The other two men must be agents. They are so engrossed in trying to find the boats that they never even glanced in my direction.* The trusted right hand of Franklin Morse straightened up and continued to walk down the line of parked cars until coming to a brown four-door sedan. Removing a key from his pocket and placing it in the lock, the man unlocked the door and got in. He reached under the back seat and retrieved the case containing the detonation device. Marcus settled into the front seat to wait. *It won't be long now!!*

Chapter Fifty

Wrightsville Beach
Just East of Wilmington

Cathy, Linda, David, Peter, and Harold Wills continued to scan the boats that were rapidly falling into line for the parade. Suddenly David yelled, "There they are!" He pointed to five boats in a row that had just pulled into position. Peter radioed the agents stationed around the flotilla route and five of them ran for the boats, as did Peter and his group.

Peter's cell phone rang just as he jumped into a small launch that would ferry him to the first boat. His supervisor's voice sounded from the other end: "We just found the bodies of Carl and another man—both shot at close range."

Wills warned us that there were to be no loose ends. I guess they outlived their usefulness. We found the boats and are about to intercept them."

As the launch pulled up alongside, Peter boarded the first boat, which was the sailboat searched previously. An agent came from below decks. "Nothing here, sir." Peter's radio crackled and the reports came in from the other boats: nothing.

The couple who Peter had met before stood in front of him. The angry wife looked at Peter and asked sarcastically, "Can we go now?" When he said yes, she spat, "Good, then get off our boat!!!" To her husband she ordered, "Get under way. We're holding up the start of the parade!"

Marcus watched as the little drama unfolded. *Everything is going according to plan.* Peter's cell phone rang again. After listening, he yelled for David, "Come on. We need to go." To another agent he ordered, "Stay with the women. Cathy—you, Wills, and Linda need to stay here and try to spot Marcus." He started to turn away, then turned back? "Are either of you armed?"

Both women opened their jackets, revealing shoulder holsters. "They gave these to us in the car when they handed us the search warrants for the boats."

Saturday Night
6:59 p.m.

It was a long flotilla parade and Marcus knew that the boats he sought would be at the end of the flotilla. "Wasn't that considerate of Mr. Morse to not want to spoil these people's total evening," he laughed to himself. "Instead of the traditional fireworks for the finale, all of these people are going to have their very own real live fireworks, up close and personal." Still, he was getting restless. He checked his watch. It was almost seven o'clock. *I think I'll get out and stretch my legs a little.*

Marcus had exited the car before the final boats came into view. "There they are!" He reached inside the car, grabbing for the case carrying the detonator. Placing it on the hood of the car, he waited patiently until the boats turned from the Intracoastal Waterway into the channel. "Wait, wait," he warned himself. "Just be patient."

Marcus watched as the boats began to drift near shore. "Good boys, you are doing just what you were instructed to do." At the precise moment, Marcus hit the detonator button. Nothing happened. He hit it again and again. Still no response. "What the?" Marcus roared.

Marcus bent over to throw the case back in the car. A pair of feminine voices spoke from behind him: "Hello, Marcus."

Chapter Fifty-One

The Intracoastal Waterway
A Few Miles North of the Wrightsville Beach Bridge

The five vessels powered by the young men left their moorings at precisely 5:40 and slowly made their way down the Intracoastal Waterway. They were to be last in the flotilla, so there was really no reason to hurry. Anthony's boat had initially been in the middle of the group but lost power and dropped back until it was next to last. His engine sputtered and seemed to be in real trouble. The other young men circled back around, unsure of what to do. Finally, Tony yelled to them to go on and not to endanger the mission. He would try to repair the engine and catch up if he could. Reluctantly, they agreed.

Tony watched his comrades once again motor toward the Wrightsville Beach Bridge now visible in the distance, then limped his boat into a nearby dock and tied up. The young man tinkered with the engine until he was sure the other young men were again focused on their task ahead. Leaping off the boat, the one time self-appointed leader sprinted toward the house attached to the dock. His only hope was to get to a telephone. He pounded on the door, but to no avail. There was no one home. He raced to the neighbor's house and again knocked desperately. When an elderly gentleman finally came to the door, Tony pleaded, "Please, sir, I need to use your phone. It's an emergency."

The elderly gentleman eyed Tony suspiciously. Looking beyond the young man, he spied the unfamiliar boat tied up at his neighbor's pier. Nodding toward it, he asked, "Is that your boat?"

"In a manner of speaking, yes."

"Having trouble with it?"

Sensing the man's sympathy, Tony answered, "Yes, sir."

The man's eyes crinkled up in a smile. He was a sailor himself. "You know what they say about boats being holes in the water that you pour money into." Unlatching and opening the door, the old sailor waved the young man in. "Come on in. The phone's in the hall. This way."

Thinking that the young sailor wanted to call someone to pick him up or provide a tow, the man gave him a phone book. Tony pretended to search for a number, but as soon as the old gentleman left him alone, dialed 911.

When the young man told his story, the dispatcher thought that the call was bogus. She was about to hang up when the caller asked for the number for the FBI or Homeland Security. *What if this kid is telling the truth?* Hesitantly, the dispatcher agreed to transfer the call. "Just a moment, sir. Someone will be with you shortly."

Tony couldn't believe it. The woman had put him on hold. After what seemed like an eternity, he was about to hang up when another voice came on the line. "My name is Emma Grayson. I am with the FBI. Would your please repeat for me exactly what you told the dispatcher." The student again relayed the events of the past few weeks, starting with his recruitment by John Marley and ending with his faking engine trouble to make this call. "Where are you?" Tony was about to yell to the old man when he noticed at stack of mail piled next to the phone. He quickly read off the address neatly printed on the top envelope. "Stay there!" commanded the woman. "I'm sending the bomb squad immediately. Once again, tell me the names of the other vessels and spell them so there will be no error." Tony did as instructed. The FBI supervisor disconnected from the boy and redialed the phone. "Peter, Emma..."

The Home of Wilbur Tide

Fifteen minutes later a small fleet of SUVs pulled into the driveway, followed by the bomb squad. Several agents along with Emma Grayson leaped out and pounded on the door. The old sailor answered the door and was roughly pushed aside. "What is this all about?" he demanded.

Emma Grayson stood in front of the gentleman and flashed her badge. "We're with the FBI. Are you Anthony Joe?"

"No."

"Where is he?"

"Never heard of him."

"Who are you?"

"My name is Wilbur Tide and I repeat my question, what are you doing in my home?"

"We received a call from an Anthony Joe a few minutes ago. The call originated from this house."

'I already told you, I don't know any Anthony Joe."

A voice from behind the man whispered, "That would be me."

Brushing past the man, the woman stated simply, "Show us the boat."

The bomb squad went immediately to the boat and disarmed the explosives.

The poor owner of the house just kept muttering over and over again, "Well, I'll be. Well, I'll be."

The Intracoastal Waterway
Just North of the Wrightsville Beach Bridge

Channing, Sokol, several other agents, demolition experts, and a Coast Guard launch that had been called in to assist, raced to intercept the other four boats just a half a mile north of the Wrightsville Beach Bridge. Through a bullhorn, Peter commanded,

"Kill your engines, drop your anchors, step away from your wheels, and put your hands on top of your heads!"

Three of the young men did as they were told and raised their hands immediately. Jonah James, however, threw his throttle foreword as far as it would go. The bow of his boat rose dangerously high out of the water. His vessel leaped and bounced over the wakes of passing boats like a dolphin at play. The Coast Guard, with its more powerful engines, raced after his rapidly fleeing boat and was quick to overtake it. With his escape route cut off and nowhere else to run, the angry young man finally killed the engine, put his hands on his head, and waited to be boarded.

After the students were taken from their boats to the launch carrying Peter and David, the demolition crews boarded the booby-trapped vessels. Luckily, the riggings were rudimentary and did not take long to disarm.

Once the explosives had been taken care of, David looked around at the dejected young men and sputtered, "These are just the little fish. It burns me to know that Franklin Morse, the real mastermind of all this, is going to go totally free because we can't tie him to anything."

Peter nodded, "Me too." He began to pace back and forth on the deck of the launch. "I think I have an idea." He quickly radioed his supervisor and explained his plan. After ten minutes he pocketed the phone, turned to the gloomy young men, and said, "Have I got a deal for you…"

Twelve minutes later Tony arrived piloting his vessel, but with Emma Grayson and her assistant on board. The FBI supervisor stepped from Tony's boat onto Peter's and asked, "Have the boys been given the offer?"

"Yes, and they readily agreed."

She snorted. "I would think so. No jail time in exchange for their full cooperation."

I still say it's worth it if we can nail this Marcus character and get him to roll over on Franklin Morse."

"That is a mighty big if, but since we found the explosives on the dredge island, my superiors agree with you. The plan now is for you and David to hide in the lead boat and other agents will hide in the rest. Anthony's boat will bring up the rear to make sure no one decides to make a run for it again."

'Let's just hope that this Marcus character panics and makes a slip when the boats fail to detonate."

Ms.Grayson and her aide got into a launch that would take them back to shore where a car awaited. Before leaving, she turned to each of the sullen young men. "With the amount of explosives that were on those boats and hidden on the dredge island, you were all going to die tonight. Whether or not you believe it, you are very, very lucky that we intercepted you. I hope you realize this by now. I also hope that the next time you are dissatisfied with something that is going on in this country, exercise your rights as U.S. citizens and vote, write your Congressman, picket in protest, do anything that is legal. Radical solutions only end in tragedy for everyone."

All the young men except Jonah kept their eyes averted. The defiant young man stared straight ahead with arms folded. David crossed and stood nose-to-nose with Jonah. "Are you agreed or not?" Jonah stared back challengingly, then, very slowly, dropped his head. "I don't have much of a choice, do I?"

David gripped the young man's shoulder. "There are always choices. This one is yours to make."

Jonah raised his head once more and, straightening his shoulders, met David's gaze. "I'm in."

Peter looked back at his boss. "We need to get going."

Their supervisor looked solemnly at the two men. "Good luck!"

With agents hidden in each boat, the young men raised their anchors and once again began their journey down the Intracoastal Waterway. They caught up to the flotilla and took their positions at the end of the line.

The Flotilla

The students, their now harmless cargo, and their hidden passengers cruised down the waterway and made the turn into the channel, floating closer and closer to the shore as they had been instructed. Even though the boys knew that the explosives had been deactivated, they were still uneasy. *What if the FBI agents were wrong and the boats could still be exploded?* They looked around nervously, keeping one eye on their navigating and one eye on the massive throngs that lined the shores. When nothing happened, Jonah, in the lead boat, finally asked David, "What do we do now?"

David, himself relieved that they hadn't been blown to bits, looked at the young man and grinned, "Finish the parade. Who knows? Maybe you'll even win a prize for your decorations."

Before the students turned their boats back into the channel, David and Peter jumped onto the nearby docks and disappeared into the darkness.

Chapter Fifty-Two

Keeping one hand on the case, Marcus turned around very slowly. "Well, well. Hello, ladies." He glanced in Wills direction. "And if it isn't the original turncoat, Harold Wills. Hello, Mr. Wills." Eyeing the gun pointed at him, he continued, "Who is the gentleman holding the gun pointed at my midsection? An FBI agent, I presume?"

Before Cathy could reply, Marcus swung the case, crashing it into the side of the agent's head, throwing him off balance. The gun flew out of his hand and into the darkness. The agent lost his footing and his head hit the pavement. He vanished into unconsciousness. In lightning quick moves, Marcus dropped the case and grabbed Cathy around the neck before Linda had time to remove her gun from its shoulder holster.

It was a standoff. Linda's gun was aimed at Marcus, but he held Cathy and now had her own gun aimed at her head. "Drop the gun or I will kill your friend."

Kill my friend and I'll kill you."

"I'm not bluffing."

"Neither am I."

Marcus took two steps back, dragging Cathy with him. "So what do you suggest?"

A slow smile spread across Linda's face. "Hey Cathy, do you still do any volunteer work?"

The woman looked mystified. "You mean volunteering at the hospital?"

"No, the stuff you do on Wednesday nights and Sunday mornings."

"Yeah, what about it?"

"Do you remember how we made a joke about it while we were in training at Quantico?"

Cathy thought for a minute then her face brightened. "Of course!"

"What is this?" Marcus demanded suspiciously.

"Cathy, show him what *this* is."

Before Marcus could react, Cathy jabbed her elbow into his solar plexus, ran her foot down the inside of his leg, and then stomped on his instep. Next she rammed her fist into his nose, breaking it. As blood gushed from his nose, she finished by kneeing him in the groin.

Linda applauded her friend. "Nicely done!"

Linda had her gun aimed at Marcus, who was still writhing around on the ground in pain when David and Peter sprinted up to them. David enveloped Linda in a bear hug before taking over guard duty of Marcus. "Are you two all right?"

"Just fine," Linda answered as she leaned against David after he had commanded Marcus to lie face down on the pavement and placed him in handcuffs.

Cathy had been ministering to the FBI agent's head wound when Peter helped her straighten up. "Is he going to be all right?"

"I'm no doctor, but I think so." Cathy rubbed her hands on her skirt. "He'll have one whale of a headache for awhile, that's for sure."

Indicating Marcus, Peter asked, "What happened to him?"

Cathy grinned. "Just like my church choir, I simply taught him to SING: solar plexus, instep, nose, groin."

Everyone except Harold Wills began to giggle. "Didn't I take you to a movie that talked about that?" asked David looking down at his fiancée. Then, as the stress and strain of the last twenty-four hours were finally released, the giggles turned into laughter and the laughter got louder and louder and bigger and bigger and turned into guffaws. The lawyer scowled at the four, fearing they had lost their minds, but they were powerless to stop. They guffawed until their sides hurt and tears rolled down their cheeks. It was uncontrollable and ended only when other agents and the EMT showed up.

Their joy, however, was short lived. Emma Grayson appeared as agents helped Marcus to his feet and prepared to haul him away. "Take him and Mr. Wills directly to my office." She strode up to Peter and the rest of the group, "I want you four downtown, immediately. This is not over, not until we get Franklin Morse."

Chapter Fifty-Three

It was well after midnight when the group gathered in Emma Grayson's office. The women had gone back to Cathy's house to take much-needed showers and to change clothes. Cathy's poor cats had been so traumatized by the last few days that she had a hard time leaving them again. "It will take weeks before they'll stay out from under the bed," Cathy complained to Linda.

"At least you are alive to help them make that adjustment."

"True."

The guys had retrieved the young men and taken them to headquarters to make their statements. Under the plea agreement, they were released into the custody of their grateful parents and were obligated to 1000 hours of community service. Each one identified Marcus and Harold Wills. They also identified pictures of Carl and Omar. Unfortunately, none of them could connect Franklin Morse.

David looked at Harold Wills. "Unless we can get someone to corroborate your story, it boils down to your word against Morse's."

"And with his lawyers, we know who'd win," added Peter, his frustration growing.

The mood in the room had grown deadly serious by the time Cathy and Linda arrived. No one said much of anything when

Marcus entered, followed by Emma Grayson. "Have a seat," Ms. Grayson ordered.

Marcus refused and instead demanded, "I want to see my lawyer!"

Peter stared eye-to-eye with Marcus. "The lady told you to sit down."

Reluctantly, Marcus did as he was told. "I still want to see my lawyer."

The supervisor placed her glasses on her nose and opened a folder. Reading from it, she said, "Let's see now, we have you on kidnapping these two women."

"You've got that all wrong. I didn't kidnap them." Gesturing toward Harold Wills, he continued, "The clown over there did that. I simply rescued them from the warehouse where he was keeping them."

Linda had heard enough. Putting her hands on her hips she demanded, "Oh, right! Then why did you tie us up?"

Marcus answered condescendingly, "It was for your own protection until I could figure out who I could trust. Then I was going to let you go."

Cathy rolled her eyes. "Sure, then what about that briefcase with the detonation devices?"

"I found it in that car. And if you check the car's registration, you'll find it is registered to one Harold Wills."

The attorney turned ashen. "What about the FBI agent you assaulted?" challenged David.

Marcus shrugged. "The man was pointing a gun at me. I had to defend myself!! The guy looked nervous. For all I knew, he might have been a trigger-happy kid. I wasn't going to take any chances."

There was a knock and another agent poked his head in the door. "This guy's lawyer is here."

Emma Grayson sighed, "Show him in."

The agent handed her a file. "This just came in. I thought you'd want to see it."

As she scanned the file, a high-profile attorney swaggered into the room and demanded to know why his client was being interviewed without him.

"Calm down. We were just having a friendly conversation," Peter said.

The FBI supervisor's face brightened. "I'm glad you're here." She looked squarely at Marcus. "We are now charging you with murder. We found a car and a gun, both registered in your name. They have your prints all over them. We just matched the bullets with the slugs we took out of two men, first names Carl and Omar. In addition, we found Harold Wills' original pictures." Emma deliberately laid each picture on the table for everyone in the room to see.

The high-profile lawyer crossed to the center of the room. "I want to speak to my client alone."

Marcus put a hand up. "That won't be necessary."

His lawyer tried to intervene. "I advise you to not say another word."

Marcus stood up. "I will not go down alone for this." He looked directly at the woman who was clearly in charge. "What kind of a deal can we make?"

The woman looked back at Marcus. "You will have to do time, but no death sentence."

Marcus shook his head. "Not good enough. My boss has connections everywhere."

Peter stepped in. "We'll put you somewhere he won't find you."

"You'll also get a new identity when you get out," Emma promised.

Marcus conferred with his attorney. The attorney sighed, "Drop the murder charges and my client will plead guilty to kidnapping." A stunned silence filled the room. "How badly do you want his boss?"

A frustrated Emma Grayson left the room. "You're slime, you know that?" David yelled as he lunged at Marcus.

Peter pulled his friend off the suspect. "Don't. He's not worth it."

The FBI supervisor re-entered the room and sat down, deliberately closing the file. "If you give us what we need, you've got yourself a deal." Marcus began to spill his guts.

At daybreak, Linda, Cathy, David, and Peter headed for the airport. They were booked on the 6 a.m. flight out of Wilmington. The four wanted the personal pleasure of placing Franklin Morse in handcuffs.

Chapter Fifty-Four

The Georgetown Townhouse of Franklin Morse
Washington, D.C.
Saturday Evening

Franklin Morse had a hard time concentrating on his dinner guests. His jovial mood subtly began to change. Flattering the ladies seated on either side of him became a tedious chore. Finally, after the main course had been cleared away and the staff was serving the dessert, he excused himself and left the room. Going directly to his chief-of-staff, he asked, "It's almost eight. Hasn't there been any word from North Carolina?"

"None, sir."

The tycoon entered the library, picked up the phone, and dialed the number to his North Carolina home. His housekeeper answered on the third ring. "Any news of interest?"   "Nothing, sir. Will you still be home at the end of the week?"

Shifting uncomfortably, Morse replied, "I may have to go to Europe for a few weeks first. I'll let you know."

The industrialist reluctantly returned to his dinner party. The final guests stayed until dawn Sunday. The man didn't think they would ever leave. As soon as the last guest pulled away from the curb, the business tycoon tried calling Marcus's cell phone. No answer. He again called his Carolina home. No one answered. *I've got to get out of here*! Morse punched in a speed dial number and woke his pilot. "Get the jet fueled and ready to go. I'll meet you at the airport in an hour."

"Where are we going?" asked the sleepy pilot.

"Somewhere overseas. I'll let you know when I get there."

"Sir, you know I have to file a flight plan." The pilot stifled a yawn.

"All right, all right, make it for Istanbul."

The pilot was fully awake now. "Istanbul?"

"Istanbul." Franklin Morse hung up and took the steps two at a time to his master suite. He pulled out his bags and was throwing clothes into them when the doorbell chimed. He could hear voices downstairs but didn't dare stop to investigate.

The butler knocked on the open bedroom door. "There are some people here to see you, sir."

"Can't you see I am busy? Tell them to come back some other time."

"I can't, sir."

Morse stopped packing and looked suspiciously at his butler. "Why not?"

"Because they are with the FBI."

Peter pushed past the butler, followed closely by David, Linda, and Cathy. "Franklin Morse, you are under arrest!" Several more agents entered the room and surrounded him. "Read him his rights!" As an agent did so, Peter took out a pair of handcuffs and handed them to Cathy. "Would you ladies like to do the honors?"

The two women looked into the lifeless eyes of the man who would have cold-bloodedly killed hundreds. "Gladly!" They spun Morse around. With two distinct clicks, Franklin Morse's hands were shackled behind his back.

Epilogue

Cathy's Living Room
Midnight
Christmas Eve

A fire crackled and snapped in the fireplace as oddly-shaped shadows danced on the ceiling. Bubbling liquid in the red and orange bubble lights reflected in the ornaments and illuminated the Christmas tree. Flickering flames from a dozen candles cast shadows of pooled light about the room. A sweet scent filled the air from the six dozen red and white long-stemmed roses standing regally in crystal vases. The only sound, other than the crackling fire, came from the stereo softly playing Native American flute music.

Peter and David stood in front of the fireplace with the minister. Both men were resplendent in their black tuxedo jackets and red cummerbunds with single red roses tucked into their lapels. David kept tugging at his collar and looking at his watch. Peter leaned toward his friend and whispered, "Stop fidgeting. Linda will be out shortly." Cathy gently pushed the holly-covered comb into Linda's hair and stepped back to survey her best friend. "You look beautiful."

The bride nervously touched the comb. "I hope the groom thinks so."

The matron of honor reached down, picked up the bouquet and handed it to her. "I know he will." Reaching for the door that led from the bedroom, she said, "Shall we?"

Peter and David gasped in unison as the ladies entered from the bedroom. The women had chosen to have the gowns from the movie

White Christmas replicated. The bride's gown was the duplicate of the one worn by Rosemary Clooney, only made entirely of white satin. The matron of honor's gown and short cape were made of red velvet with white fake-fur trim, exactly like the one worn by Vera-Ellen.

Linda carried a bouquet of miniature red and white roses interspersed with baby's breath and assorted greenery. Instead of flowers, Cathy carried an old-fashioned white fake-fur muff with a touch of holly at the corner. Both women looked stunning.

The wedding ceremony was simple, yet elegant and beautiful, just like the fairy tale most women dream of. The groom chose to give his bride two wedding bands, one a plain band of white and yellow gold to always be worn, and another band of tiny diamonds to be worn on special occasions. The bride gave the groom a matching band of yellow and white gold, only with one small diamond in the center. As the couple exchanged traditional vows, all four of them had tears in their eyes. The past week had been yet another reminder of how precious life is and what a rare gift it is to find true love.

Even though the official reception would not be until Christmas Day, after the ceremony, Cathy served a small cake. Peter toasted the happy couple with champagne. By the time the new Mr. and Mrs. Sokol changed their clothes and departed for the hotel, it was well after two o'clock in the morning. Peter helped Cathy wash and dry the champagne glasses and cake plates. After the last of the dishes were put away, Peter took Cathy's hands. "Can we talk for a few minutes?"

Cathy tried unsuccessfully to stifle a yawn. "Can it please wait until tomorrow? I'm beat, and tomorrow, I mean later today, I promised Linda that I would take the flowers and her gown over to the hotel. I also promised to oversee everything at the reception." She eyed Peter's now slightly disheveled appearance. "Don't forget that you still have to wear your tux tomorrow—I mean today."

Dejectedly, Peter glanced down and tried to smooth the wrinkles out of his shirt. "I guess I better get going then." He kissed Cathy on the cheek. "Merry Christmas."

Christmas Afternoon
Royal Sea Shell Resort

The wedding reception was in full swing when David cornered his best man. "Now that it's been almost fifteen hours since the ceremony, I can definitely attest to the fact that marriage the second time around is great!! You ought to try it. Are you still carrying that engagement ring in your pocket?" Peter reluctantly produced the tiny velvet box. "I can't believe you still haven't asked Cathy to marry you! You've been carrying that ring around for weeks. What keeps stopping you?"

Peter looked embarrassed. "Between that Morse business, Cathy having to grade finals, and your wedding, it's just never seemed like the right time. I started to ask her last night after you two left, but she was tired."

David inclined his head toward Cathy, who stood talking to Emma Grayson. "No time like the present."

Peter inhaled a big breath. "Wish me luck." He casually joined the two women.

Cathy turned to Peter. "Emma has great news. Franklin Morse is going away for a very long time."

The FBI supervisor nodded. "That man will never again see anything except through bars or barbed wire. And the agent who was hurt the night of the flotilla is fine and has returned to duty. "

"Thank goodness, it's all over," sighed Cathy.

"I'm really glad," murmured Peter. "Now if you will excuse us, I really need to talk to Cathy alone." Guiding her by the elbow, Peter started for the door to the outside terrace.

Sensing what was to come, Emma's eyes twinkled merrily. "Of course."

Peter led Cathy outside and down onto the beach. Kicking off her shoes and picking up the bottom of her dress, she asked, "Where are we going?"

The dashing agent looked down at the woman he loved. "Nowhere. I just wanted us to be alone."

"Why, for Heaven's sake? This is a party!"

Before she could say anything further, Peter Channing bent down on one knee, reached into his pocket, took out the ring box, and opened it. "Cathy Cleveland, will you marry me?"

There was a moment of absolute silence as if even the waves were waiting for her answer. Suddenly, in one fluid movement, Cathy pulled Peter up onto his feet and leaped into his arms screaming, "Yes! Yes! Yes!" Thunderous clapping erupted above their heads as the bride, groom, and rest of the wedding guests applauded from the hotel's outside balcony.

The couple turned toward the sound. Cathy gazed up at the crowd through a glowing sheen of happy tears. Waving to their best friends, the newly engaged couple shouted in unison, "Merry Christmas!" The groom raised his champagne flute in a toast: "A happy new year to us all!"

Their world once more seemed a beautiful and happy place...but is it destined to stay that way? Only time will tell.

Printed in the United States
47667LVS00003B/277-300